Savage
TITAN

E.V. OLSEN

Tropes and Trigger
WARNINGS

Tropes

SEXUAL AWAKENING, OPPOSITES ATTRACT, POSSESSIVE MC, BULLY MC, HURT/COMFORT, GRUMPY/SUNSHINE, SIZE DIFFERENCE.

Trigger Warnings

THIS BOOK CONTAINS SOME THEMES THAT MAY BE DISTRESSING TO READERS INCLUDING:

DESCRIPTIVE SEX SCENES, IMPACT PLAY, VIOLENCE/BULLYING, ROUGH SEXUAL PLAY, HOMOPHOBIC TERTIARY CHARACTER WHO MAKES HOMOPHOBIC REMARKS (APPEARS TOWARD THE END), MENTION OF CHILDHOOD PHYSICAL ABUSE, EMOTIONAL ABUSE BY A TERTIARY CHARACTER TOWARD THE END.

Alexei

CHAPTER ONE

A packed crowd fills Crestwood University's ice arena, affectionately nicknamed "The Colosseum." They roar as I skate onto the ice, a thunderous welcome that sends electricity coursing through my veins. Our fans always turn out in droves, and I gorge on their energy, letting it fuel the simmering darkness within me, a beast awakening from its slumber.

My eyes take in the sea of gold and maroon—our team colors. Banners wave, faces painted, and signs held high proclaim their devotion to the Titans. These people, they're here for blood as much as they are for hockey. They want to see bones crunch, blood spill, and spirits break.

And who am I to deny them?

I circle the ice during warm-ups, my skates carving precise lines into the pristine surface, and catch sight of my reflection in the plexiglass. Dark eyes stare back at me, cold and focused. My left cheek bears a slight scar, a reminder from my father to stay focused on my goals.

To be the best. To dominate. To win.

It's also a reminder, if he ever touches me again my mother will end his life. And no one—not even my father—fucks with Yulia Petrov.

My cousin Viktor slams his goalie stick on the ice, one of his pre-game rituals to feed the madness glinting behind those ice blue eyes. The sound echoes like a war drum signaling the coming onslaught. "Let's give these fools a nightmare they'll never forget."

Some days I can't understand why he put his NHL career on hold to play at the university level. He's an amazing goalie, was even drafted. But for some reason, my cousin wants to also study Chemistry or something.

And part of me is thankful for it because we get to spend more time together. After his family left Russia to move to America a few years ago, I missed having him around. And I also worried about who would watch his back. My cousin may be unhinged, but he's also openly gay, and some hockey players have an issue with that.

Jackson Reed, my roommate and one of our centers, glides up beside me. He flashes his signature smug grin, all teeth and no warmth. "I'll have their winger begging for mercy by the second period."

I snort, amused but not about to be outdone. "We'll see about that. Bet he doesn't last past the first."

As we line up for the opening face-off, I lock eyes with the Aviators' dumb schmuck new winger. He's fresh meat, probably still high on the adrenaline of playing his first game in our arena. Poor bastard has no idea what's coming.

He glares at me over our winger's shoulder. "Russian ox! I'm gonna plow you into the boards all night. You won't know what hit you by the final horn."

"Big words. Will you back them up or crunch when I crush you like a bug?"

I bare my teeth in predatory excitement. The monsters are out to play. This fool has no idea the hell about to be unleashed on him.

The puck drops and the Aviators take possession, but only for a second. I'm on the pathetic bug, smashing his body into the boards.

The crowd erupts into feverish cheers.

They know what I can do.

What I live for.

I gain possession of the puck, then pass to Jackson.

He catches it and effortlessly weaves through the opposing players with a graceful agility that belies his imposing stature. His powerful strides carry him toward the Aviators' net.

As Jackson winds up for a slapshot, the air crackles with anticipation. The sound of his stick connecting with the puck echoes through the arena, sending a shockwave of excitement through the crowd. The puck soars toward the net, a blur of speed and precision.

The Aviators' goalie, caught off guard by the sheer force behind Jackson's shot, desperately tries to make the save. But it's futile. The puck finds the back of the net with a satisfying swoosh, and the arena explodes.

I turn to Jackson as he skates by. "Nice shot. Think that one's begging for mercy already."

Jackson turns toward the Aviators' goalie, a wicked smile spreading across his face as we head back to the bench for a line change. "Just warming up. Gonna make that net his personal hell."

Connor Walsh, our captain, fist bumps us as he hops over the boards toward center ice. "Keep this up, and we'll be bathing in their tears by the third."

"Told you the winger would break." I jut my chin at the fool heading back to his own bench. "He's favoring his left knee."

Jackson turns to me, raising a brow. "But he's still kicking. You going soft?"

The snarl that leaves my lips is dark, viscous. A warning. He might be my friend, but he should know better than to test me. No one is truly safe from the beast that lurks beneath my skin, not even those closest to me.

Except for Viktor.

The annoying pest is the family favorite, and both my mother and aunt would end my existence if I hurt him seriously. Like the time we were drinking that summer he came back to visit after moving. My cousin accidentally caught fire. It was his fucking fault, yet I also got punished for it.

But he came out with a good luck charm he carries everywhere.

We skate out for the second period and my eyes immediately lock onto my target. He's back on the ice, fire flashing in his eyes when he catches me staring.

He wants revenge.

Good.

I give him a little wave—taunting and provoking. His lip twitches into a scowl. Perfect.

The puck drops and I muscle toward him, prowling like a predator sensing weakness. He tries to stay on his feet but I bodycheck him hard, savoring the satisfying crunch of impact and relishing his cry of pain as he crumples to the ice.

The refs' whistles shrill through the air, but I'm not finished. Not by a long shot. I yank him up by the collar of his jersey, his feet dangling inches off the ice. Leaning in close, I murmur threats in Russian, my voice low and menacing. "Give up or I'll end you right here."

He snarls and spits in my face. Fool. Doesn't he know that only feeds the monster? With a growl, I slam his head against the ice, feeling a sick satisfaction as his body goes limp.

That's enough to cause both teams to engage.

"Fuck, yeah." Jackson launches at a player, his fist swinging over and over. Blood sprays everywhere, as for sure he broke the other player's nose.

Of course, my actions don't go unpunished. The refs kick me out for the rest of the game, but I can't bring myself to care. As I skate off the ice, head held high, I know I've done my job. I've set the tone, broken our opponent's spirit.

And when the final horn sounds, it's no surprise we've emerged victorious. What a way to start the weekend.

Eli

CHAPTER TWO

The Monday morning sun filters through the towering windows of Crestwood University's food court as I weave through the maze of tables toward my friends, balancing a tray loaded with a steaming mug of coffee and a sad-looking blueberry muffin.

Winston looks up from his phone, his brow furrowed. "Did you just tumble out of the laundry basket or is this a new fashion statement?"

I plop down across from my two best friends, running a hand through my chaotic dirty blond hair. "Oh this? Bedhead Chic is the latest trend or haven't you heard? Seriously though, I stayed up way too late working on sketches for a new sculpture."

A common occurrence, especially when my brain decides to host a midnight party for a million ideas. I like to get them all down on paper, even if most end up looking like abstract blobs in the morning.

Not that I would've gotten much sleep last night. The dorm was a zoo, which always happens after one of Crestwood's sports teams has a game. I'm not into sports, so I have no clue who played, but judging by the drunken celebrations echoing through the halls, Crestwood must've been the winner.

I could barely hear myself think over the chants and cheers. At one point, I swear someone was trying to start "The Wave" in the corridor. Same thing happened this weekend too. Guess that's the price I pay for going to a school that's well known for its athletic program.

Sasha leans forward, her dark curls bouncing. "Ooh, for the exhibition next month? Let's see!"

My fingers hover over the zipper of my backpack as my cheeks flush. "They're mostly just doodles."

Winston huffs, shaking his head. "Your *doodles* are like mini masterpieces. And you know we're your biggest fans."

I pull out my sketchbook, then flip it open as Sasha and Winston crowd around. My teeth sink into my bottom lip as they peer at the page filled with rough outlines of human fingers in various positions.

Winston's head tilts as he takes in the drawing. "Is this about your sister?"

"Yeah. I'm trying to capture how she experiences the world without sound, you know? The isolation, but also the unique perspective she has."

My older sister is extraordinary. She's my hero, my confidante, and the first person I came out to. I'd been worried, not about how our parents would react, but how the rest of the people in my world would. That was the day she shared how isolating her world could be, even when surrounded by family.

Sasha squeezes my arm. "She's going to love it."

"I just hope I can figure it out in time. It's the concept that's calling to me more than the others. Besides, Professor Hartley's standards are sky-high."

She rolls her eyes. "Please, you're her star student. She practically swoons every time you turn in a project. Now, can we talk about something more important? Like the fact The Grind has a new barista who looks like he stepped straight out of a Calvin Klein ad?"

I snort into my coffee. "And here I thought you were just going there for the superior espresso."

"Hey, a girl can appreciate art in all its forms," she says with a wink.

Winston pokes at his scrambled eggs as he stares at me. "Speaking of, when are you going to get back out there? It's been a year since The Great Tinder Catastrophe."

I groan, burying my face in my hands. "We agreed never to speak of that again. It's like the Voldemort of my dating life."

My friend laughs, taking a bite of his eggs, which have to be cold by now. After he swallows, leans back in his chair. "All I'm saying is, you can't let one bad date ruin your love life forever."

I peek out from between my fingers. "One bad date? Let's not forget about the fact he referred to me as his 'curious experiment' while groveling to his wife. You know, the wife who knocked on the window of his car while he had his—Well, you get the picture."

Sasha purses her lips, drumming her nails against the table. "I still don't understand why you wouldn't let me punch him when we ran into him at the pizzeria."

I pick off a piece of my muffin and toss it at her. "Because I don't have the money to bail you out of jail."

"Well, I could've thrown my milkshake at him."

"I happen to like milkshakes too much to let them go to waste."

Sasha reaches across the table and pats my arm. "Just promise me you won't become a hermit, okay? Your artistic soul needs inspiration."

"Oh, please. I'm so not into the whole 'muse' thing." I take a bite of my muffin and roll my eyes.

While my sister is the source of inspiration for my latest piece, it has more to do with the fact I've actually witnessed some of her struggles. And dealt with my own sense of isolation at times.

But the idea of one person inspiring my creativity . . . it's never been a belief I connect with.

Winston shrugs. "You're telling me you wouldn't be inspired by Sasha's 'work of art' barista?"

Sasha slaps his arm. "Hey, I called dibs. He's mine."

I chuckle, shaking my head. "Not my type."

Winston quirks a brow. "What is your type exactly? I know you were dating what's-his-face for a few months when we first got to Crestwood."

Dropping the rest of my half-eaten muffin onto the tray, I take a sip of my now lukewarm coffee to wash it down before responding. "I'm not sure what my type is. Or if I even have one. I guess when the time is right someone will sweep me off my feet."

Sasha groans. "And if there ever was a Prince Charming, you'd be the one to snatch him up, leaving the rest of us with toads."

Winston purses his lips. "At least you get toads. I don't even exist on anyone's radar."

I drink the last of my coffee as my two friends argue over how Sasha's tried to set Winston up before but he always chickens out at the last minute. As I set my empty mug down onto the tray, my phone chimes. I grab it and yelp. "Crap. I've got to run. Composition class starts in ten minutes."

"Ooh, with the dreamy Professor Evans?" Sasha waggles her eyebrows.

I roll my eyes as I gather my things. "Have you learned nothing from my married guy experience?"

"Didn't say I would date him, but I certainly wouldn't be missing his class." She smirks as she looks at me. "Oh, is that why you're in a rush?"

"Please. You know I have to maintain my grades to keep my scholarship."

"But isn't statistics the subject you struggle with?" Winston's mouth twitches as if fighting off a smile.

"You two are incorrigible. All right, I'm off to compose myself—literally. See you guys later."

After depositing my tray, I exit the dining hall and speed walk toward Ormsby Hall. Professor Evans hates tardiness almost as much as he hates misplaced modifiers, and I have no intention of earning his wrath today. Not when he admonishes tardy students in front of the class, as if his little power trip is going to make them respect him more.

If there's one thing I can't stand, it's bullies. And I've never been one to back down from a challenge, especially when it comes with a side of arrogance.

Alexei

CHAPTER THREE

I shut off the near freezing stream of water, simultaneously shaking my head to dispel droplets from my hair. Today's schedule is nearly identical to every other—wake at 4:30, eat breakfast, practice, Titans team meeting, shower, classes, strength and conditioning training, shower again, homework, then sleep.

Hopefully, the latter will be uninterrupted tonight.

Doubtful.

Not when Jackson insists on barging into our room well past midnight, most likely coming back from some pointless late-night hookup, making all kinds of racket. And no matter how many times I've cursed him out this month alone to be quiet, he keeps doing it.

Next step—smother the fuckface with a pillow.

Of course, the stupid prick shoots me a shark-like grin as I walk through the locker room, towel around my waist. "What's wrong? Didn't get enough shut eye, Sleeping Beauty?"

My lips press into a thin line as I shove him out of the way to get to my locker. "Lucky you're my friend or I'd break your wrist, Sweetie Pie."

He grabs my throat, eyes dark and deadly. "Watch it, Petrov."

I step into it, grinning like a fucking Cheshire Cat. We're the same. Psychotic assholes. Jackson, however, seems to get off on the violence. Like it's some type of foreplay.

Can't wait until he meets his match. Going to be someone tough, hard, lethal. The type who'll shoot him in the leg because they had a bad day and he breathed too loud. Anything else would be too boring for my friend. Bet that's why he goes through girls the way people go through tissues—blow into them, then toss them out.

I don't understand the girls here, how they throw themselves at everyone like they have no respect. They are so different from my mother, aunt, and Viktor's sister. The women in my family would rather cut their tongues out than be desperate.

Coach Nieminen crosses his arms and glares at the both of us. "Unless the two of you want to sit in the stands this weekend, you boys better knock it the fuck off."

I turn and scowl at the old man.

"Don't call me boy again." My voice is low and full of venomous promise. Don't care if he's a former Stanley

Cup champion, I'll smash his face in, especially when the damn phrase comes out all demeaning like the way my father says it.

Coach ignores me, focusing on one of our newer teammates. He is used to our threats and pays us no mind. I bet he's secretly just like us. Definitely played like us when he was younger.

After grabbing my clothes, I get dressed and snatch my book bag, making sure to give Jackson the finger as I walk out of the locker room. The motherfucker may be my friend—I use the term lightly—but in the end he's just another rung to climb to the top.

Or so my father's taught me about everyone.

Everyone serves a purpose. If they don't, they're useless.

Even me.

My fingers coil around the strap of my bookbag, my jaw clenching so hard, I might crack a few teeth. I'm glad the old man is an ocean and fucking continent away from me. While the pressure of making it to the NHL drives my days, at least the suffocating blanket of his existence is a bit lighter being far from him.

I've only been in this country two years and was forced to live with his family when Viktor's mom offered to take me in. But my father and my aunt loath one another. Not sure my aunt ever liked him, but when he called spat at

Viktor calling him a faggot when we were thirteen, my aunt nearly blew his head off.

I can still picture the incident, the barrel of her 9mm in his mouth . . . if only she had pulled the trigger.

The alarm on my phone goes off. Twenty minutes to cut across campus and make it to class. I hate Mondays. The one day the lecture hall is the farthest from the rink. Fortunately, most dickheads have the common sense to get out of my way. And anyone who doesn't know me gets plowed into.

Their fault.

If they don't know better than to make way for one of the star defensemen of the North Shore Titans, then that isn't my problem.

I push the door open to Ormsby Hall, my sneakers hitting the tile in perfect cadence. Only, as I turn the corner of the cream-colored hallway, something small collides into my chest. The impact doesn't faze me, and I have the pleasure of watching the little mouse of a man land on his ass.

He shakes his dirty blonde head as he tries to gather his supplies strewn across the ground. The situation is mildly amusing and I lean down, pretending I'm about to help him but, really, it's just for show.

I get eye level with him, and his face is all flushed, his cornflower blue eyes darting around at the other students who can't seem to look away from his little drama. He cracks a hopeful smile at me, probably thinking I'm here to save the day.

Yeah, right.

I smirk back just to mess with him, the corners of my mouth stretching slowly, deliberately, letting a hint of sadism seep through.

He reaches out for one of his books, but I snatch it right out of his grasp. *"Mastering Fundamental Composition,"* I read off the cover.

Funny, I've got the same one in my bag.

I stand to my full height, which is easily half a foot taller than him. "Maybe you should learn how to walk properly, or you could just stick to crawling."

His smile drops, and I can practically see the gears turning in his head, trying to figure out his next move.

He gathers the rest of his stuff in a rush, then scrambles to his feet. He looks up at me, sighing when I don't hand over the book.

For a moment, he bites his bottom lip, then meets my gaze straight on. "Can I have it back?"

With him standing right in front of me, I notice he's not exactly as scrawny as I first thought, but still, he's no match for me. I'm broad, sharp, all about muscle and power. He, on the other hand, is leaner, softer—sure, maybe athletic but still just another pushover.

Literally.

I could shove him back down if I wanted.

And you know what?

I do.

Then I fling the textbook farther down the hall. "Next time, watch where you're going."

I stroll past him and make my way to class.

Of course, by the time I get to the lecture hall, the only seats left are upfront. But I'm on time.

Barely.

The professor throws a shitfit anytime someone's late, stopping the lesson and everything to admonish them.

Fucker after my own heart.

Gotta love degrading those beneath you.

No sooner do I open my notebook to a blank page when something catches my attention in my periphery.

"Hey, asshole!"

My eyes narrow immediately as I look up at the boy from the hallway, who's now standing at my side. My lips part slightly at his goddamn audacity.

"Not sure what crawled up your ass, but don't ever throw my things again."

My nostrils flare as I snap my pencil from squeezing it. Who the fuck does he think he is talking to me like that? "Better move before your neck is next."

His eyes widen for a second before narrowing, a lopsided smirk on his face as the seriously dumb fucker drops into the seat right next to me and opens his notebook.

My fists clench, and I'm about to grab this tool by the collar and fling him five rows behind me when the professor cuts me off. "Mr. Petrov, I suggest you focus on the lesson unless you intend on sitting in the stands for the next game."

As if that would ever happen.

But still. Not taking any chances. My goal is to get signed by an NHL team.

And the little mouse next to me isn't a rung to step on.

So, he's worthless.

Not worth another second of my attention.

Eli

CHAPTER FOUR

By the time I make it back to my dorm, my legs are like lead and my brain's nothing but mush. I dump my bag on the floor, then face-plant onto my bed, letting out a groan that's muffled by my pillow. The familiar scent of laundry detergent wafts up, offering a small comfort after the day I've had.

Especially after my run-in with the douchebag. Just my luck we happen to share the same class, not that I remember seeing him. Maybe he normally sits in the back.

And what was with the whole pencil snapping thing? The sharp crack still echoes in my ears.

Maybe sitting next to him wasn't the brightest of ideas. Not because he intimidated me—please, I've dealt with bigger jerks than him—but because I couldn't concentrate for the hour and a half I was stuck in class. There's also the embarrassing way my skin had flushed, heat prickling under my collar, and I swear I never sweated so much in my life.

Not that the grumpy bastard was any better. Like every stroke of his pencil was louder than it should've been. My one consolation—he had nothing else to write with, so he had to sharpen the pencil he snapped.

I snort, the image of him struggling with that tiny nub with those large hands flashing through my mind. He looked comical. I couldn't help but chuckle out loud, which was a mistake.

Because he slapped my books onto the floor.

Again.

A knock at the door pulls me out of my pity party. I haul myself up, then trudge over to the door, opening it. Sasha stands there, armed with a giant bowl of popcorn and a grin that could light up a stadium.

"Wipe that frown off your face. It's movie night." She pushes past me and makes herself comfortable on my bed. Once settled, she pats the spot next to her, inviting me to join. "How was your day? Learn anything fascinating?"

I flop down beside her and grab a handful of popcorn. "Only that people suck. I had a run-in with some jerk today. Literally."

Sasha's eyes widen, and she sits up, her full attention on me. "What? Who was it?"

I shrug, trying to downplay the encounter even as my heart rate increases. "No idea. Professor Evans said something about the guy sitting in the stands during the next game, so I'm guessing he's on one of the sports teams."

She rolls her eyes, a familiar gesture that speaks volumes about her opinion of jocks. "Ugh, typical. The fucking athletes think they own the place. Did you at least give him a piece of your mind?"

A smile tugs at the corners of my mouth. "I may have called him an asshole and told him not to throw my stuff again."

Her eyes widen. "*You* cursed at someone?"

I roll my eyes and wave a dismissive hand. "Wasn't one of my better moments. But then I sat right next to him in class. He did nothing but scowl and mutter under his breath like a grumpy toddler. He even smacked my notebook onto the floor."

She laughs, her eyes sparkling. "Sounds like a real charmer."

I cross my arms over my chest. "Oh, he's charming all right. About as charming as a root canal."

"Maybe he was flirting by knocking your books to the floor, like he's in kindergarten. You know athletes aren't always the brightest." She giggles and nudges me with her elbow. "What does he look like?"

"Tall, dark, and douchey."

I chew on the inside of my cheek. I doubt the douchebag was trying to flirt, not after threatening to snap my neck. But Sasha's offhand comment about intelligence bugs me, especially when one of the smartest people in my Art History class is a lacrosse player. And Dante is one of the sweetest people.

She quirks a brow, head tilting slightly. "Okay, dark as in mysterious and brooding, or dark as in 'I eat puppies for breakfast'?"

"Somewhere between. He's got this sharp jawline and dark eyes. Like, really dark. Almost black. And there's this scar on his left cheek. It's not huge, but it's noticeable. Makes him look kinda . . . dangerous."

Her mouth falls open for a second before she smirks, a mischievous glint in her eye. "That's a lot of detail to notice, Eli Holmes."

Heat spreads across my face as I look away. "Only because I sat next to him."

"Uh, huh. So you didn't find him hot?"

I shove too much popcorn into my mouth, bits falling out past my lips when I try to chew. But she continues to stare at me, until I swallow and finally answer. "He's an asshole, that's all that matters."

Sasha laughs and hops off the bed to grab the remote from my desk. "There you go, cursing again. Alright, enough about Mr. Tall, Dark, and Douchey. It's movie night, and I've got the perfect horror flick picked out."

I grab the third pillow on the bed—yeah, I like pillows—and hug it. "Please tell me we're not watching with clowns again. I had nightmares for a week last time."

"No clowns, promise. But there might be a creepy doll or two."

I shudder, my arms tightening around the pillow. "Great, because possessed toys are so much better."

"Ooh, can you imagine if they had a possessed vibrator?"

I stare wide-eyed at my friend, because now that she's conjured the image in my mind I can't *not* think about the idea.

"You should see your face right now." She laughs so hard she snorts. "Bet if we Googled it we could find something like that."

"No!"

I'm sure we would find some weird stuff if we actually looked, and the last thing I want is to be afraid of the only source of physical pleasure I currently have.

"Anyway, I was thinking we should go out sometime soon."

I stare at her, blinking. "Go out? Like, to a party?"

She shoots me an incredulous look, like I've grown a third head. "Yeah, why not? Or we can go to a bar."

I wrinkle my nose, not exactly thrilled at the prospect of spending a night surrounded by a bunch of drunk strangers. I'm more of a stay-at-home-and-watch-movies kind of guy. "We have class the following day."

"So, don't drink. And we don't have to stay out late." Sasha gives me her best puppy dog eyes. "Come on, Eli. It'll be fun. Plus, we can convince Winston to come with us. You both need to get out more."

I sigh, running a hand through my hair. My friend won't take no for an answer. And it's not like I have anything better to do. "Fine. But only if Winston definitely goes too. I'm not going to be the third wheel while you flirt with every guy in sight."

"Deal." Sasha stretches out on my bed like a cat in the sun, basking in her triumph, then she hits play and the movie begins.

Maybe a night out won't be so bad. I've been working myself too hard between classwork and sculpting.

What's the worst that could happen . . . I end up dancing on a table?

Alexei

CHAPTER FIVE

Viktor, Jackson, and I walk up the stone pathway toward the large double oak doors of Walsh's parents' place. Or estate. The fucking gargantuan house looks more like a modern castle and it's packed already.

Walsh's parties draw more motherfucking students than most frat parties, even on a Wednesday night. Most of the people here are smart enough to keep their drunk asses away from us.

Unless we're in need of a toy or three.

Nothing like a mouth to rail to take the edge off, something new I learned could help with my stress. Never had much time for sex before, not with my father controlling every minute of my life.

"Ouch, fuck, you crazy bastard!"

Leave it to my fucking cousin to palm some kid's head and smash it into the wall for almost running into him the moment we walk through the door.

Viktor ignores the outburst, looking at me instead. "Dumbass just learned his lesson. See me coming, move."

We head into the large family room with ceiling to floor windows. Walsh is sitting on a sectional, a glass with amber alcohol in hand as some redhead kneels between his legs and sucks his dick. "Nice of you assholes to make it."

I walk to the bar and pour myself some Johnny, then flop onto the couch. "Fucking Jackson and his damn hair routine took forever."

"Think I want to look like I just rolled out of bed?" Jackson kicks my foot to get by.

I snort. "Well, you did."

Viktor leans against the bar. "How many did he fuck at once this time?"

I hold up three fingers.

Zach Knight, our other top defenseman, strolls in, shaking his head with a grin as he comes over. "Surprised your dick hasn't fallen off yet," he says as casually as asking about the weather.

My cousin and Knight stare at each other as Knight takes a seat next to me. Something happened between them at some point, but Viktor won't talk. And Knight keeps his business to himself. He even becomes threatening if someone pries too much.

But what I don't understand is why my cousin is always tasting Knight's food.

I turn back to Walsh and watch as the girl sucks him harder. What I would give to have my cock in a warm mouth right now. Besides this show, I walked in on Jackson . . . more like, cockblocked him and kicked the girls out so we weren't late.

Hate being late.

Not that I'm into parties. Hockey's my life. But these things do provide me with what I need on occasion—a few drinks and a tight hole to rut to relieve some stress.

I grab my half-hard dick and give a little squeeze. Luckily, some brunette in a skintight black dress that barely covers her ass looks my way. I raise my glass and beckon her over.

She smiles, not that I care. I'm too busy deciding what hole of hers I want to use. And when she sits on my thigh instead of on the couch, I decide on her pussy.

But no sooner do my fingers start trailing up her inner thigh when I spot that motherfucking nobody from Composition class. The asshole who, instead of fearing me, sat right next to me, even laughed at me.

Kid's out of his mind.

If the dumbass professor hadn't asked to speak to the little mouse after class, I would've crushed the rodent in the hallway.

My eyes narrow, both in anger and to focus. He looks out of place. Most people dress up, but this idiot is wearing a T-shirt under an open button-down, loose fitting khakis, and a pair of Vans.

I clench my jaw and continue staring. He's going to pay for yesterday's antic. Maybe sex isn't what I need. It's a different kind of toy.

A different kind of prey.

A little mouse that will be lucky to make it out of here alive.

"Who's that?" Knight asks.

I roll my head from side to side, cracking my neck. "Someone who's going to wish he never ran into me."

Jackson's now also looking, as is my cousin. Walsh is too busy fucking the redhead's throat brutally.

My gaze refocuses on the little mouse who is surrounded by two other nerds. At least his friends seem to understand the concept of a party, grabbing drinks and chugging them. He just stands there, hands in his pockets and a stupid half-smile on his face.

As if he's honoring *us* with his presence.

Knight gives a predatory laugh, like a serial killer who's asked if he's about to disembowel the person he's captured. "Need help destroying the mundane little meat suit?"

"No." The little mouse is no threat. Plus, Knight and I have a different way of torturing people. "I got this one."

Viktor sits up, a dramatic whine leaving his lips before he pouts. "You better not leave me out. I could use some fun."

Ignoring my cousin, I shove the slut off my lap and she lands on her ass.

"Hey!"

I just step over her. Does the dumb bitch really think I care about her complaints? My mother has more self worth in her pinky toe.

"Asshole!" A second later she squeaks and I look over my shoulder.

Knight's got his fingers in her hair, yanking her head back. "Watch who you call an asshole."

I roll my eyes when she readjusts herself between his legs, then continue walking, eyes fixed on the irritating freckled face of my target. This is all on him. He entered my domain.

The fool is now holding his red solo cup carelessly, making my job *so* much easier. I pick up my pace and as soon as I'm close enough, I knock the cup forward.

Not a flashy move, just enough to get the game rolling.

I chuckle low and threatening as red stains the front of his T-shirt, his face and hair also getting splashed by whatever the hell he was drinking.

Ugh, not surprised he's drinking some low-end spiked punch.

"What the fuck!" He looks down at himself, body frozen still, eyes wide as red liquid drips down the length of him.

"Oops. Didn't see you there."

All around us, people scatter. But a few remain, including his friends, and though the female is staring daggers at me, she keeps her trap shut.

The other nerd looks like he might drop dead from fear.

Little Mouse, however, looks like he's about to punch me in the face. I almost want to laugh, his expression is so cute. As if he could hurt me.

"What is your prob—" He takes a deep breath and looks away. "You know what? You're not worth it."

He turns his back on me.

He turns his fucking back on me.

The satisfaction from a few moments ago melts away like heated wax. This mother fucker.

"Where the fuck do you think you're going?" My voice comes out as a booming growl, like I'm a fucking devil or some shit.

But he just keeps walking, blatantly ignoring.

"Eli!" his female friend calls out, then chases after him, the other close on her heels.

Eli.

My fingers clench and unclench. I'm going to strangle Eli, make him wish he never stepped foot on Crestwood University's campus, that he never crossed my path.

And I'm definitely going to make him regret that holier-than-thou attitude because he obviously didn't get the memo that the Titans rule this school.

Not some punk nobody.

Just like in hockey, it's time to read the play, then wait to take advantage when the opportunity arises.

So, I hide in the crowd, stalking him, waiting for the right moment.

And, eventually, it comes.

Good thing this is Walsh's house, and I'm familiar with the layout. Eli's making his way toward the bathroom.

I'm right behind him, just far enough away but still close, like one car tailing another.

Just as he walks into the bathroom, I push him forward, slam the door, then grab his collar and shove him up against it.

His eyes go wide, brows lifting high on his head as he turns a bit pale.

Perfect.

I crowd him, my fist tightening in his shirt. "I'm not finished with you."

Eli swallows, his Adam's apple bobbing as he reaches up, placing his hands on my chest, trying to push me away to create space. "Look, I don't know who you are or what the hell you want but—"

"You've got to be kidding me. You don't know who I am?" I widen my grin, baring my teeth. "Well, let me introduce myself. I'm Alexei *fucking* Petrov. Son of Vladimir and Yulia Petrov."

I wait for the look of recognition, but it doesn't come.

"Okay? And? I'm Eli Holmes . . . er, son of Marcus Holmes?" He closes his eyes for a moment, then exhales a deep breath before re-opening them and staring me dead in the eye. "I don't care if you're some entitled ass rich nepo baby or whatever is fueling that massive ego of yours. Nothing gives you the right to treat people like this."

Mother. Fucker.

I growl, stepping closer, pretty much erasing any distance between us as I loom over him, intentionally breathing into his face to intimidate as I thrust him against the door again.

He lets out a small gasp from the force and shivers slightly. The confidence on his face breaks and his lips part slightly as he gazes up at me.

My eyebrows knit together when his pupils dilate, breath coming out in shallow rasps, eyes still locked onto mine.

I growl, lip twitching up into a partial sneer. "What the fuck are you looking at?"

He doesn't respond, only drops his gaze to my mouth, then bites his bottom lip as red splotches stain his cheeks.

My body tenses, my jaw hanging open slightly. Out of all the reactions I've received from anyone I was about to beat the shit out of, this one's new.

And when he releases the faintest of whimpers, my grip weakens.

Without my fucking consent.

Electricity sizzles down my spine to my groin, and suddenly I realize how close I am to Eli, how it's not just my breath hitting his face but his hitting mine as well, how our bodies are pressed firmly together, nearly every inch touching. Every cell pulses in time with my heartbeat, and my eyes travel back down to his mouth where he's chewing on his pink, swollen bottom lip.

Wonder what that would feel like between my *teeth.*

What the fuck!

I let go of the front of his shirt, then push him sideways and I take a step back.

Flinging open the bathroom door, I practically sprint down the hall, fingers raking through my hair and pulling at the roots, especially when I realize I'm rock hard.

What the fuck is wrong with me?

Eli

CHAPTER SIX

I trudge out of Art History class, head swimming, unable to recall a thing about whatever the lecture was on. And the charcoal still life I did looks like trash—totally phoned that one in.

No mystery why I'm distracted though. Ever since last night's insanity, my thoughts have been a hot mess, and my friends won't stop grilling me about what happened with Alexei in the bathroom.

Sasha thought he'd hurt me.

Besides being about seven inches taller than me, the aggressive asshat is built like a steam engine and manhandled me like I weighed nothing. I'm not exactly weak. I work out and have more lean muscle than bulk. Still, I'm tiny compared to him.

But when Alexei roughly pinned me up against the door, the hint of whisky on his breath invading my nose, my previous distaste for the asshole evaporated.

As did all my pride and self-respect, apparently.

My hands tighten around the strap of my backpack and I flinch when recalling that stupid whimper.

Like . . . What. The. Actual. Hell.

I should've been punching him, kneeing him in the balls, not whimpering like a needy idiot.

But I wasn't prepared for the rush of heat that flared through my body. I can't believe I got hard.

So embarrassing, and why I'm never going out again. Nope, it's movies and popcorn only for me from now on.

Except I wasn't the only one who got turned on.

By the time I stumbled back to my dorm last night, my mind was still spinning and my body . . . well, let's just say it hadn't gotten the memo about hating Alexei. But there was no way in hell I was going to do anything about that, not when he was the cause. So, I'd yanked out my phone, desperately searching for a distraction. And what better way to kill any remaining arousal than by researching the king of entitlement himself?

Turns out Alexei Petrov isn't just some random douchebag athlete. He's a hockey player, the Titans' star defenseman. And when I texted Sasha this morning to see if she has more info, she virtually shit herself.

Supposedly, her ex-boyfriend was beaten to a pulp by Alexei last year. Can't say I'm surprised. But she also informed me the hockey team is pretty untouchable since half of their parents, Alexei's included, are billionaires who donate to the school.

The same families that also run Rosewood Bay and the incorporated village's private police department.

Must be nice to have that kind of money.

Not really, not if it makes you a prick with no basic regard for people's feelings.

I hate people like that, those who think they can buy their way out of consequences. Normally, if I come across someone like that, I fight back. I don't roll over and play dead.

My voice deserves to be heard.

Only last night, it wasn't my voice that did the talking. Nope. It was the dumb sex sounds that filled the room, even if they were barely a whisper.

What I hate even more is that his aggressiveness turned me on.

Excessively.

In all fairness, he is sexy. With dark hair, a jawline so sharp I could cut my hands on it, thick lashes framing intense brown eyes that almost look black, and his criminally smooth Russian accent—the man's a walking hard-on.

Still, he's an asshole, just like the Tinder jerk. And that should negate how good he looks.

Frustratingly, it doesn't.

What I can't make sense of is why he suddenly sprinted away. It seemed so out of character for the brute he is.

Maybe I'm not the only one who was blindsided by whatever the hell happened between us. Because, let's face it, we were both hard. There's no denying that, even if it makes zero sense. And if I'm being honest with myself, which I'm not sure I want to be, I felt like I was two seconds away from kissing him. Or maybe being kissed. Or not.

The thing is, I'll never know.

Fate seems to have other ideas because the moment I turn the corner of Ochre Hall, one of the many 19th century mansions the University utilizes, the stupid man I can't get my mind off walks out of the University's sports complex.

And in typical Eli Holmes pigheaded fashion, I can't leave well enough alone.

So much for heading to the cafeteria for lunch.

"Hey!" I call, running across the neatly trimmed lawn, doing my best to catch up to his ridiculously long strides. He doesn't even look my way so I try again. "Alexei! Hey, dickhead. Wait up!"

Why do I always curse when it comes to this guy?

He stops so suddenly, I almost run into the big bastard.

Again.

Because it seems the universe finds it funny to have us crash into one another.

"What the hell did you just say?" I take a step back as he looks me up and down, his face turning red, the vein in his temple sticking out. "Need a dirt nap? Would anyone even miss you if you disappeared?"

I keep my tone cordial, if not a little forceful. "Oh, please. Spare me your tantrum. It's anything but flattering. I just want to talk."

His nose scrunches up but he doesn't break eye contact. "I don't talk to nobodies like you."

I bite my tongue at that last insult because, deep down, it hurts. Maybe because he is somebody, at least to this school. And I'm . . . not.

Pushing down the feeling of inadequacy, I straighten. "Why not? Don't want to ruin your asshole reputation by acting decent? Look, I wanted to talk about what happened last night."

He steps forward so fast, it's as if he's going to lunge at me and rip my throat out. But I stand my ground, though I do have to tilt my head back a bit so I can match his stare.

He grins, cocks his head to one side, and says in his thick Russian accent, "Oh, yes. I too wanted to talk to you about that."

I'm caught off guard. "Wait, really?"

"Well, less talking and more punching your ass into a permanent fixture in the pavement."

I roll my eyes hard and sigh heavily before returning his smirk. "Very mature. Wait, is that what last night was about? Were you trying to intimidate me into sleeping with you?"

"What?" He practically splutters. "I am not—I like girls! I wasn't trying to have fucking sex with you!"

I don't miss how he avoided directly saying "gay."

And now his sudden exit makes sense. But if he's still threatening to beat me up, I'm not letting him off easy either. "Could've fooled me. What with how you looked at me . . ."

Alexei spins on his heels and stomps off. And, stupidly, I follow.

My shoulder brushes against his as he stares ahead, ignoring me. "Why'd you follow me into the bathroom anyway?"

He whirls around, his hand coming around my throat, squeezing hard. "Do you want to die?"

I grab onto his wrist and try to pry myself free, trying to ignore the fact my dick is getting hard.

"You're nothing but a little mouse who needs to be squashed."

My eyes narrow. "Why because I'm gay and you can't deal with the fact you got turned on?"

Alexei immediately releases me, then shoves me so hard I stumble back and fall. "Shut the fuck up."

I swallow past the growing lump in my throat, my eyes stinging as I fight to keep the tears from forming. He just stands there, staring at me, his chest heaving with each breath.

Then he turns once again, and runs away.

Like he did last night.

Alexei

CHAPTER SEVEN

I storm away from Eli, my heart pounding like a fucking jackhammer. My fists are clenched so tight, I'm sure my nails are drawing blood from my palms. How dare that little mouse insinuate I have an issue with him being gay.

Bullshit.

Not after those worthless fucks cornered Viktor when he was twelve, beating him while spewing their homophobic trash. Our own goddamn teammates, ambushing him after practice.

I'll never forget walking in on that shit show—Viktor fighting off seven pieces of human garbage. My cousin was outnumbered but it didn't matter.

We fucked them up good—my cousin bit a chunk out of one asshole's face. I shattered more noses than I could count. By the time the coaches showed up, those fuckers were a bloody mess on the floor.

And while my cousin insisted he was fine, his eyes were dead for months after. A muscle near my eye twitches.

I swore I'd never be like those dickheads, never hurt someone for who they want to fuck.

But the little shit was right about one thing—I can't deal with getting hard over him. Can't get his goddamn lips out of my head. Even now my cock is swelling, just like it had when I wrapped my hand around his throat.

"Fuck!" I growl and kick a stray pebble on the path. It skitters across the pavement, and I wish I could kick something harder, something that would make a satisfying crunch under my foot.

I've never looked at a guy like that before. Only ever bothered with girls when hockey allowed. So why the hell can't I shake the image of Eli's flushed face? Why do I keep replaying how his breath caught when I pinned him?

Maybe it's because the little shit stands up to me, even when I threaten to break him. It's infuriating. He's a nobody, just some art student who should piss himself at the sight of me.

But he doesn't.

Nope, that stupid mouse ran right up to me, challenging me until I'm the one who ran away.

I walk faster, my breaths coming out in ragged gasps. It's all messing with my head, even fucked with practice this morning.

"Hey, durak, what's got your panties in a twist?"

I glance over my shoulder to see Viktor jogging toward me with that stupid grin on his face. The one that usually means he's about to be a pain in my ass.

"Nothing. Fuck off." The words come out as a low growl.

He snorts, falling into step beside me. "Yeah, and I'm the Queen of England. Spill it, asshole."

I lengthen my stride, but the persistent fucker easily matches me.

"Let me guess, has to do with why you ran out of Connor's party like your ass was on fire?"

My feet stop moving and I whirl to face him, getting right in his space. "You going to tell me what happened with Knight?"

Viktor's smile vanishes, lips pressing into a thin line as he brushes past. Yeah, the one fucking topic that shuts him up. Pisses me off too because he won't talk to me.

"Well, get your shit together. We're playing Harvard this weekend. Can't have our star defenseman all wound up, leaving me exposed." He taps his chin, grinning. "Then again, I'm so fucking awesome I don't need you."

The familiar banter loosens something in my chest. I roll my eyes, landing a half-hearted smack to the back of his head. "Fucking child."

"Ugh, you sound like my dad. Speaking of, Mom wants to know when you're coming over for dinner."

"Asking or demanding?" Like I need to ask. My aunt and mother are cut from the same damn cloth. Their 'invites' are as optional as breathing. "What's she cooking?"

My cousin snorts. "You know as well as I do we have a cook. But there'll be Pelmeni, or I'll throw a bitch fit about how she doesn't love me anymore."

"Dramatic asshole."

He whines, throwing his hands up in the air. "Not my fault. This organic chem bullshit is destroying me worse than when we tried to outdrink Uncle Yuri. These reaction mechanisms? It's trying to read your chicken-scratch handwriting after a dozen shots of vodka."

I rub my temples, fighting a headache. This idiot's too much sometimes. "So what, your average dropped to ninety percent? Cry me a fucking river."

Viktor huffs. "Don't insult me, asshole. It's at ninety-three percent."

This fucking guy. Gets drafted, has a brain that could solve world hunger, and bitches because he's not perfect. Meanwhile, I'm busting my ass for B's and he acts like the world's ending.

For a blissful moment all the confusing shit I've been dealing with fades away.

But as we near the dorms, my phone vibrates. I pull it out, cursing under my breath. My father's name lights up the screen like a goddamn warning sign, stomping out the peace I just started to feel.

It's a text, short and to the point, with an image of my latest hockey stats attached. "Stop embarrassing the family with your mediocrity."

My jaw clenches, throat constricting. The phone nearly cracks under the pressure of my grip as I shove it back into my pocket.

Viktor's eyes narrow. "Let me guess. My delightful uncle? Mom should've blown his fucking head off."

I grunt in response. But this time my father has a point. Or at least his words remind me what I should be focusing on.

Hockey. Success. Proving myself. It's what I need to do to achieve my dream.

I roll my shoulders back, chin lifting. Time to get my priorities straight and forget about the boy from Composition, that almost-kiss, and all the confusing shit he stirs up.

Eli

CHAPTER EIGHT

I'm running late, and not by accident. I lingered at my dorm this morning, dragging out every little task—brushing my teeth, fixing my hair, retying my shoes—anything to delay walking into Composition class and seeing *him*.

Taking a deep breath, I push open the heavy wooden doors and step into the lecture hall, immediately spotting Alexei in the back row. He's sitting in the back, arms crossed over his broad chest, looking like he's just waiting for an excuse to tear someone apart. Charming, as always.

"Mr. Holmes." Professor Evans's sharp voice cuts through the air. "How kind of you to grace us with your presence."

My shoulders hunch as my cheeks heat. "I'm sorry, Professor. I—"

"Perhaps next time you'll consider the value of your classmates' time, not to mention mine."

I mumble another apology and hurry to an empty seat near the front. Of course, as I sit, I glance back at Alexei, like the glutton for punishment I am. He's staring right at me, his gaze so intense I have to look away, my heart pounding.

Great job, Eli. Real smooth.

As Professor Evans begins the lecture, my pen moves across the page of its own accord. I glance down to find I've sketched a familiar jawline, sharp cheekbones, intense eyes. My breath catches, and I quickly flip to a new page.

"Mr. Holmes."

My head snaps up, my stomach plummeting. Oh, this can't be good.

"Perhaps you'd like to share your thoughts with the class since you seem so absorbed in your notebook."

I sit up straight, acutely aware of the weight of everyone's stares. The back of my neck prickles, and I know without looking that Alexei is watching too, probably enjoying this.

"S-sorry, I—" I flip through blank pages as if I've got some genius hidden in there. Come on, brain. Don't fail me now.

I swallow hard, my mind racing for an answer that won't make me sound like a complete idiot. "I was just . . . jotting down some ideas about the, uh, symbolism in the poem we discussed last class."

Professor Evans arches an eyebrow, clearly not buying it. "Really? And what symbolism would that be, Mr. Holmes?"

Sweat beads on my forehead as I grasp for an answer that at least hits somewhere in the ballpark. Or the parking lot outside. "The, um . . . the use of nature imagery to represent the speaker's emotional state?"

"Interesting, considering we haven't discussed any poetry recently. Perhaps you'd benefit from paying more attention and less time on your . . . artistic endeavors."

A few snickers ripple through the room and I sink lower in my seat, wishing I could disappear. Or spontaneously combust. Either would be preferable at this point.

"Now, as I was saying before Mr. Holmes so kindly volunteered to demonstrate the importance of active listening . . ."

My palms grow slick as I fidget with the edge of my notebook, foot tapping restlessly against the floor. The fabric of my shirt clings uncomfortably to my back, and I keep my gaze fixed downward.

When class finally ends, I bolt for the door, desperate to escape. But as I round the corner into the hallway, a large hand grabs my arm, yanking me to a stop. Because why would the universe let me escape that easily?

I spin around, already knowing who it is before I see him. Alexei towers over me, his grip on my arm tight enough to bruise. My heart races as I stare up at him. "What do you want?"

"I want you to stop looking at me," he says in that deep Russian accent.

My breath hitches. I should be terrified, but all I can focus on is how close he is, how the heat radiates off his body and into mine. "I wasn't."

Liar, liar, pants on fire.

"Bullshit."

"You know what? Fine, I was." My eyes narrow as I tilt my chin up. "But you were staring at me too."

Alexei shoves me against the wall, his massive body caging me in as he leans close, his breath hot on my face. "Listen carefully, little mouse. Stay the fuck away from me. Stop staring. Stop following me. Or I'll make you regret it."

"Why does it seem like it's your personal mission to make my life hell?"

He chuckles, low and menacing, before patting my cheek with enough force to make me wince. "Don't flatter yourself. You mean nothing to me."

Then he's gone, leaving me breathless and trembling against the wall. My skin tingles where he touched me, and I'm horrified to realize I'm half-hard in my jeans. What is wrong with me?

A few strangling students from class filter out of the lecture hall, staring at me. Between Professor Evans and now Alexei, I've provided my classmates with enough entertainment for today. But there's still one problem. I need to pass Composition 101 to keep my scholarship, so I have to resolve this issue with Alexei.

By the time I exit Ormsby Hall, Alexei's already halfway across the quad. Before I can think better of it, I run after him.

"What part of 'stay away from me' did you not understand?"

"The part where we're in the same class and need to figure this out." I'm practically jogging to keep up with his ridiculous stride. "You can ignore me all you want, but we're stuck in this class together. So unless you plan on dropping out, we're going to have to deal with this."

He doesn't respond, and frustration bubbles up in my chest. His dismissive attitude stings more than I care to admit, and I want to grab him, shake him, make him acknowledge me as more than an insignificant speck he can just brush aside.

Before I know it, we enter Young Hall and holy crap. My feet slow and I spin, carefully taking it all in. It's like a hotel. Well, really it's just another 19th century mansion Crestwood uses, but this one's for residential living.

While I don't consider myself someone who needs luxury, the history is awe-inspiring. It's a far cry from my dorm building, which is pretty much what you'd find on any college campus.

Hanging from the ceiling in the center of the main room is an extravagant chandelier with four oversized leather chairs beneath it. Large arched windows line the upper walls and the staircase has that old, sturdy wood feel.

Alexei walks up the stairs and I follow after him, because apparently, I've lost all sense of self-preservation. He heads down a hallway lined with candelabra wall sconces, then stops at a door.

Great.

I've followed the big bad wolf right to his lair. But this whole "Eli doesn't exist" game isn't funny anymore. "I don't get it. Why do you hate me so much? Is it because we almost kissed? Or the fact we were both—"

The world around me turns into a blur, a sharp pain erupting throughout my entire scalp. I trip over my feet as I'm tugged forward by my hair. But instead of falling to the ground, I collide into Alexei.

He lets go of my hair and shoves me away, mumbling something I don't understand as he slams the door shut.

I take a moment to compose myself after being pulled and pushed and shoved and, by every definition of the phrase, thrown around. And Jesus, why do I like it so much?

"Shut the fuck up about your damn delusions."

This jerk nearly ripped my hair out and he thinks I'm going to cower. No way.

I raise an eyebrow and place a hand on my hip. "Delusions? Oh, you mean my delusions about how your breath got all hot and heavy, and you kept leaning in closer and closer while your hands gripped my shirt? Or that you were as hard as—"

"Not another fucking word!"

When he stalks toward me, my confidence evaporates, and I step away until I back into the wall. I push my hand against his chest, attempting to create some space between us, but he's solid, unyielding—a force of nature.

Alexei yanks my hair, tilting my head back so my eyes meet his. "I told you to shut the fuck up."

I can't tell if the heat now burning its way through me is from Alexei's body, the flush of my face, or a combination of both. "Make me."

What the fuck, brain? Or mouth? Whichever one of you thought that was a good idea.

Alexei's grip tightens, his anger palpable. His eyes are so dark they look black. I swallow hard, wondering how many broken bones I'll end up with. But instead of hitting me, his lips crash into mine.

I let out a muffled sound of surprise as our mouths sloppily meld together, teeth knocking against one another briefly.

My mind goes blank and my body slack.

He bites down on my bottom lip and I whimper at the pain, my eyes closing and letting the heat coursing through my veins override any protest.

I grip his shirt tightly while our bodies press against each other as his tongue forcefully enters my mouth.

Our kiss turns greedy and vicious. My fingers slide up into his hair as he presses me harder into the wall. When he bites my lip again, this time drawing blood, I whine and buck my hips into him as my fingers tug at his dark, curly strands.

He grabs my wrists and pins them above my head.

I break the kiss briefly and try to wrench my wrists away. "H-Hey!"

Alexei only tightens his grip and dips his head down to nuzzle against the space between my shoulder and neck. His hot breath skates across my skin for a split second before he bites down.

Hard.

I throw my head back, hissing at the pain. But pleasure shortly follows when he sucks and licks at the spot.

My dick is straining against my jeans and aching, desperate for more friction. So, when our dicks finally touch and he starts grinding himself against me, I purr.

Like actually purr.

Alexei's grunting like a man possessed, driving his hips into mine with a force that lifts me up onto my tiptoes.

We both move faster, harder.

Out of control.

"Alexei . . . more. . ." I push my whole body into his, my voice practically a sob, every part of me on fire. "More."

His teeth sink into my earlobe and he lets out a low growl, thrusting into me like a feral beast.

My hands try to yank free as I writhe against him, my moans loud and filling the room. "Alexei . . . I'm . . . Fuck, I'm coming . . . I'm coming in my pants."

What the holy hell?

Whatever self-degradation about filling my pants just passed through my lips only makes the pulses of cum shooting all over the inside of my boxers that much stronger.

Alexei grips my hip so hard with his other hand, his fingers practically impale my skin while he continues humping against me until his eyes squeeze shut and a loud groan rips from his throat as his body shudders.

When he stills, I rest my head back against the wall, both of us panting as we try to catch our breaths.

Alexei releases his hand from my hip and for sure he's left bruises. He takes a small step back, his eyes finally opening. But instead of looking at me, he stares at the floor as if in a daze.

"Hey, you okay?" I keep my voice soft.

But he stays silent.

I pull my hands free from his grasp and they shake slightly as I reach up to brush some loose curls of sweaty dark brown hair away from his face. "Alexei?"

"Leave."

But when he continues to avoid looking at me, I run my fingers through his hair in an attempt to comfort him.

Is he a bully?

Yes.

But I basically had sort-of-sex with the guy and based on what he said before, how he only likes girls, this is all new for him.

"If you want to talk about it—"

"Leave now." When he finally looks at me, it's through narrowed slits filled with a dangerous glint.

"Okay." I slide sideways against the wall, making my presence as small as possible. Respecting his wishes for privacy, I walk out the door.

Putting aside all the shit he pulled to humiliate me, I'd say it was the best sex of my life.

Well, sort of sex.

What is dry humping even considered?

And being restrained . . . it was mind blowing, every last second of it.

If only it wasn't with the savage Russian hockey player who most of the time seems to want to punch my face in for just existing, I'd explore it more.

Eli

CHAPTER NINE

I stare at the lump of clay, willing some sort of inspiration to strike, but my thoughts keep spinning back to the same bewildering preoccupation—dry humping Alexei Petrov, the apparently not-so-straight hockey player I've developed a crush on.

It's been five days since getting off together. Five days of wondering if it actually happened or if I hallucinated the whole thing. Five days of replaying every moment, every touch, every heated breath in my mind. The weight of his body against mine, the intoxicating scent of his skin, the way his fingers dug into my hips – it all feels so vivid, yet so surreal.

I poke at the clay absentmindedly, the *Shape of You* playlist drifting from my earbuds doing nothing to spark creativity. With a heavy sigh, I lower my head into my hands.

I can't stop thinking about his hands on me, his mouth crushing mine, his hard dick pressing against mine. The memory sends another shiver down my spine, goosebumps rising on my arms despite the warmth of the studio.

But anxiety is also present because I can't shake the lingering concern for him either, can't stop wondering what's going through his head, especially when he's skipped Composition class on Monday and today, as if he's avoiding me.

Is he freaking out? Regretting what happened? Or is he just as confused and overwhelmed as I am?

Maybe I should be happy I'm not a target of his bullying anymore, that things have gone back to the way they were before I ran into the brute.

Fingers suddenly dig into the back of my neck, wrenching me around. I yelp, my heart leaping into my throat as I rip my earbuds free. And there he is—the star of my daydreams and nighttime activities—glaring down at me with those dark brown eyes.

"What the hell!"

Alexei glares, his hand still clamped on me. "Who the fuck do you think you're talking to?"

I slap his hand away, trying to ignore the way my skin tingles where he touched me. "You, jackass."

"Watch your damn mouth." He steps closer, looming over me. The scent of his cologne fills my nostrils—a heady mix of cedar and something spicy that makes my head spin. His eyes are full of danger, but there's something else there too. "You better not have told anyone about what happened. If you did . . ."

"I'm not that kind of person." I try to refocus on my work, rather than continuing to argue, especially when it's about his sexuality. It took *me* a darn long time to say it out loud, and I have the most supportive parents in the world.

Paper rustles behind me and I whip around to find him flipping through my sketchbook, through the anatomy studies I've been working on for Figure Drawing. There are some pretty detailed nude sketches in there, and the thought of him seeing them makes my face burn.

"Don't!" I launch myself at him but he dangles it out of reach, his height an unfair advantage. He continues perusing each page while easily fending me off with one hand.

"Give it back, you towering dick!" I hop up, swiping at the book. My fingertips brush the edge, but he pulls it away at the last second.

He spins away, now wholly immersed in my drawings. With a huff, I fold my arms across my chest and wait. "Why do you have to be such an asshole?"

He ignores me, continuing to do what he wants. Like always.

I watch him, studying the way his brow furrows in concentration, the way his fingers delicately turn each page. It's a side of him I haven't seen, and it's oddly captivating.

After a few moments, he gently sets the book down, then picks up my mini sculpture, turning it around in his large hands. He raises one dark brow at me. "What's this?"

"Just a model."

"It looks boring. Ordinary." He juts his chin at my sketchbook, open to a rather detailed rendering of the male pelvic bone. "Not like those."

My jaw actually drops for a split-second. A compliment. From Alexei-fucking-Petrov? I shake it off quickly, trying not to let it affect me. But I can't deny the warm glow of pride that blooms in my chest. "Thanks. My scholarship doesn't allow for ordinary. Or failure. If I mess up one important project, it could ruin my whole academic plan going forward."

I tap my pencil eraser against the table. Why am I telling him this? I guess mutually coming in our pants together warped my brain a bit. More than a bit.

"Hockey is much the same." He clears his throat, looking away. "If I don't impress the scouts, my career ends before it begins."

"But you can still get a job, finish your degree. Not like me, my parents can't afford the tuition." I shake my head and snort, bitterness creeping into my tone. "Must be nice to have everything handed to you. Bet your dad could buy a team and get you on if it's that important."

Wrong thing to say.

Alexei's entire demeanor changes, his body tensing like a coiled spring. He grabs my chin, forcing me to look into his narrowed eyes, now filled with a dangerous spark I've never seen.

"You think my life is easy? I earn my place on the ice every damn day." His chest heaves, face turning red. "Don't act like you know me."

I've pressed a button, one I didn't mean to.

Now I feel two inches tall.

"I'm sorry." The words come out barely above a whisper, but I mean them.

He releases my chin but doesn't step away. He just stands there, tension radiating off him in waves. When he finally meets my gaze again, something vulnerable yet defiant stares back at me.

I offer a weak smile, trying to diffuse the situation. "So . . . you don't get to automatically play all the time even though you're on the team?"

Alexei lets out a deep sigh, then drops onto the stool beside me. He's all coiled power and frustration, his muscular frame too big for the small seat. "No. Playing in games is earned. Even as a professional. No guarantees."

"That's a lot of pressure."

"Didn't make the draft either. Crestwood is my only chance to make it to the NHL."

"Why didn't you make it?"

His expression turns cold, stoic. "Was projected to be a late round pick, and with the shit going on in my country, scouts were skittish. Broke my leg, and since they weren't sure how it would heal or affect my development, ended up undrafted."

He's right. I don't know anything about him . . . or what it's like for any athlete. Or how a broken leg can decide your whole future.

Or even how a country you come from can decide your fate.

I lightly bump his shoulder. "Well, looks like you're not the only asshat in the room. Seems I've got my own implicit biases running rampant."

The corner of his mouth quirks up, only a faint amount, but it doesn't matter. Now I want to see this asshole fully smile and be the one to put it there.

Alexei

CHAPTER TEN

I'm not one to talk about personal shit. Definitely not about how my broken leg knocked me out of the draft. No one was sure how it would heal or affect my development. I fucking fought tooth and nail to get back to where I am now.

But with Eli . . . somehow the words just tumble out. And it doesn't make me want to smash his pretty face into the wall afterward.

Much.

Could do without the sympathetic look. It's part of why my ass skipped class the past few days. Thought maybe this weekend's games would clear my head, help me refocus on what's important.

No such luck.

And it pisses me the fuck off because my desires are out of control.

Every second I'm not focused on hockey, my brain dwells on how Eli's body felt pressed against mine. Or those little whimpers he makes.

All of which lead to me constantly jerking off.

I've never looked at a guy that way before. Never been attracted to anyone the way I'm attracted to him.

If it was just sex, fine. But it's not. I got all itchy and shit the moment we got back to campus and went right to *his* damn dorm because I needed to see him.

Thank fuck I snapped out of it.

I only got angrier—with myself, with this uncontrollable need, with the chaotic shit that little mouse is stirring up inside me. So I said fuck it and skipped Composition. Not just because of Eli, though.

Usually, I get off on Professor Dickhead tearing into students. But when he went after Eli last week? I wanted to rip the fucker's throat out with my bare hands. And watching Eli shrink in his seat? I snapped another goddamn pencil, imagining how satisfying it'd be to jam the pieces into the professor's beady little eyes.

So, yeah. It's more than sex since I started giving a shit about anyone else going after Eli.

But not seeing him for an additional three days sucked and I didn't understand why I was keeping myself from what I fucking want.

And that's why I'm here now.

Eli smiles at me, easy and open. "You know, you're almost tolerable when you're not acting like an entitled dickbag."

"Adorable? You're fucking kidding, no?"

He mimes zipping his lips, blue eyes dancing. "Secret's safe with me. Won't tell a soul you can be *adorable*. God forbid I ruin that reputation of yours." He leans in slightly, voice lowering. "I kinda like having Not-A-Total-Asshole Alexei to myself anyway."

The way he looks at me with heat and mischief makes my breath catch. I adjust myself, jeans suddenly too tight. Eli doesn't miss it, gaze dropping to my groin. He drags his full bottom lip between his teeth and my fucking dick twitches.

My heart thunders as he slowly and deliberately drags one fingertip along the inside of my wrist. Sparks skitter up my arm from the featherlight touch, and my jeans grow even more uncomfortable.

"Eli. . ." My voice is a near growl, but he only smiles wider, like he knows exactly how he's affecting me, how he's slowly unraveling my self-control one teasing caress at a time.

"Yes?" He blinks up at me all faux innocence.

But I see the need there, one surely matching my own, and in one quick motion, I grip his slender throat and yank him up. He gasps, arousal lighting up his face.

"Still think I'm tolerable?" I hiss the question, our mouths a breath apart.

He trembles against me but tilts his head, baring the smooth line of his neck. "Very. . ."

Lust surges hot through my veins. I squeeze gently, but hard enough to feel him swallow, and my eyes trace the movement down his neck to the bruise from where I had bitten him.

Possessiveness rears its head, fierce and unfamiliar. What is it that makes me yearn to own him in every way imaginable? Is it a way to gain control back, or is it because he makes me feel alive in a way I never thought possible?

Doesn't matter why I want to make him mine, only that I do, and I will.

Gripping his sweater, I tug the collar to the side, exposing more of his flesh. He whimpers softly as I lean down and scrape my teeth across the mottled skin before biting down.

Mine.

This little mouse belongs to me.

Someone clears their throat loudly. "Some of us have work to do."

Eli slumps, cheeks scarlet while he tugs his sweater collar back in place as a snarl lodges in my throat.

I grab Eli's bag and shove it at his chest. "We're leaving. Now."

He nods, and I wrap one big hand around his slender bicep and steer him out the door.

Outside the moon hangs high and heavy above us as we make our way across campus, the cool night air doing nothing to curb the fire raging inside, the fire that feels as if it'll char me to pieces.

I glance over to find Eli watching me, teeth chewing at his bottom lip, and I steer us toward the tree line skirting the dorms. We slip into the dark copse of oaks, and I spin and pin him to the nearest trunk, his bag thudding to the leaf-strewn ground.

My hands bracket his head when our tongues collide. He drags blunt nails down my chest as I rock my hips forward, erection thick and insistent against his thigh.

Eli sucks my tongue, then grazes it with his teeth. I growl into his mouth, my fingers twisting cruelly in his dirty blonde hair and I force his head back, exposing the enticing line of his throat.

Such an impudent mouse deserves to be thoroughly marked until the whole goddamn world knows precisely who he belongs to.

I bite his tender skin, painting the pale canvas with vivid red and purple as he cries and arches into my mouth, ratcheting my lust higher.

His hands claw at my shoulders now, fingernails biting through my shirt. The sting sets my nerves ablaze and I rut against him, cock achingly stiff.

I pull back just enough to rasp in his ear, "Time to put those pretty lips to better use."

A ragged moan slips free when his knees hit the ground. I make quick work of my fly, groaning as my erection springs free.

Eli licks his lips, wide eyes locked on it. "You're . . . huge."

"Stop talking and get my cock nice and wet." I fist myself loosely, bumping the leaking tip against his parted mouth. "Show me what a good little cocksucker you can be."

He sucks me down without hesitation, licking skillfully along my length. I bite back a loud groan, tangling my hands in his hair as I guide his head to match each rough snap of my hips.

"Just like that."

His fingers creep up my thighs, inching dangerously close to my asshole. This is new to me, and while my cousin is gay, I haven't exactly figured out what I'm comfortable with.

I tighten my grip on his hair. "Did I say you could touch me?"

Eli's cornflower blue eyes meet mine as he pulls off with a wet pop, lips swollen and chin glistening. The picture of debauched temptation.

I tap his cheek with my wet cockhead, leaving sticky trails on smooth skin. "Hands to yourself unless I say otherwise. Got it?"

He nods.

I guide myself past his beautifully stretched lips and set a savage pace as soft palms slide over my hips.

"Such a useful mouth." I pull his face flush to my pelvis, fucking deep into his throat, his wrecked whimpers vibrating along my length.

My orgasm hits like a freight train, pleasure cresting sharp and hot. I come down his throat, then pull back enough to paint his face.

He blinks up at me, dazed, coated in my cum.

"My perfect little mess. Fucking beautiful." I stroke his swollen lips, collecting the last pearly drops. "Don't waste any."

His pink tongue darts out, lapping my release from my fingers without hesitation.

My gaze travels down his body to the outline of his erection, and I let out a low growl, my hands itching to touch him.

I lift Eli effortlessly back to his feet and spin him to face the tree, pinning his hands overhead with one of mine.

The other deftly opens his jeans just enough to free his cock. There's no hesitation, no anxiety when my fingers wrap around the hot, rigid flesh.

And when he whimpers, I only want to touch him more. To bring out more of those noises.

"Oh, fuck yes . . . Alexei please . . ."

I nip the shell of his ear, stroking him roughly. "You wanna come for me, Solnyshko?"

"God, yes . . . feels so good . . ."

When his pretty cries ring out into the quiet night, I release my hold on his wrists and press two fingers to his panting mouth. "Get 'em nice and wet for me."

He latches on instantly, tongue swirling. After a few seconds, I withdraw them and reach down to trace slick circles around his hole.

"Ah! Fuck . . . fuck yes . . ."

I continue to tease and poke, not only so he whimpers more, but to figure out how comfortable I am with it all. But when I breach the furled rim with one long finger and he keens, desperate, fucking himself back for more, a smile tugs at my mouth. "What a needy little slut you are."

I slide a second finger alongside the first, then I twist my wrist, pressing deeper.

He clenches down. "H-how do you . . . Oh, God. Do that again . . . How do you know. . ."

I huff out a laugh. "Fucked a girl in the ass once, Solnyshko." I bite his shoulder hard enough to mark him. "Now shut the fuck up and focus on coming for me."

It only takes a few more strokes inside and out before his sharp cry rings out into the night as he spills over my fist, warm and wet. I milk every last drop from his trembling body.

When he finally goes lax, I withdraw my fingers, then lift my coated hand to his mouth. "Clean up your mess, Solnyshko."

That tongue eagerly gets to work, lapping his cum from my skin. My renewed erection nudges against the cleft of his ass and I groan.

Voices in the distance remind me we're less than subtle right now, so I tuck him briskly back into his jeans, then palm his softening cock.

"This is mine now, understand?" I give a pointed squeeze and he whimpers. "No one else gets to see or touch what belongs to me."

He nods. "Yours."

Eli

CHAPTER ELEVEN

Sprawled on my bed, I sketch idly while my roommate rushes around getting ready for class. Jamie's in the sciences and has evening classes for labs. We're like two hermits who accidentally ended up sharing a cave—both quiet, always buried in our work, and we get along mostly because we're too busy to bother each other. Either he's off to the library or I'm holed up in the studio, covered in clay. But overall, he's nice and that's what's important.

Alexei on the other hand is far from nice. But there's something about him that keeps drawing me in. And the raw, primal way he fucked my mouth . . . my brain short-circuits every time I think about it. Which is embarrassingly often.

God, it was intoxicating. And I'm not usually one for the whole submissive thing, but apparently, my body didn't get that memo. I mean, I can't even explain why it turns me on so much. Maybe I should start a pros and cons list: "Reasons Why Being Manhandled by a Russian Hockey Player is Surprisingly Hot."

And don't even get me started on his possessiveness. The way he grabbed me and declared ownership? It should freak me out, but instead, it's just … confusing. Because I have no idea what it meant. Like Are we together? Or am I just a casual hookup with a "no touching" sign for everyone else? Meanwhile, he gets to do whatever—or whoever—he wants?

Great.

Now I'm imagining him with someone else. Cue the jealousy I definitely shouldn't be feeling.

I shake my head, trying to dislodge the mental image. I have no idea where we stand, and it's driving me up the wall. To make matters worse, he was absent from Composition class Friday and today.

For hockey.

Not that I looked up the Titans schedule during Composition 101 or anything. Nope. Definitely didn't get called out by Professor Evans. Again. Maybe I should stop sitting up front.

But going four days without seeing him is torturous. And it's not like we exchanged phone numbers or anything.

A knock at the door jolts me from my spiral of overthinking. Jamie answers it, and his face goes so pale I half expect him to faint on the spot. "Uh . . . Hi?"

Alexei in all his brooding glory, looms in the doorway. Without a word, he shoves past Jamie into our room. Real charmer, this one.

I hop off the bed, rolling my eyes. "You know, a simple 'hello' works wonders. You should try it sometime."

Alexei just grunts, his dark eyes fixed on me.

Jamie looks between us like he's watching a tennis match played with grenades. "Uh, I'm just . . . gonna go. To class. Now."

As soon as we're alone, Alexei stalks towards me, and suddenly I'm having trouble remembering how to breathe. His large hand cups me through my jeans, his eyes narrowing. "Has your roommate seen what belongs to me?"

Here we go again with the possessiveness. I should be offended, really. Instead, I'm embarrassingly turned on. When I don't answer, he slaps my face—not hard, but enough to sting. The sharp sensation only heightens my arousal, and I whimper, involuntarily grinding against his palm.

He chuckles, a low, dark sound that sends shivers down my spine. "I didn't realize how needy you are, Solnyshko. Now answer my question."

I shake my head rapidly. "N-no."

Alexei squeezes, and suddenly I'm clinging to his biceps, moaning in a way I'll definitely be embarrassed about later. When he releases me, I try to collect myself, which is easier said than done because my brain has turned to mush. "W-why did you stop by?"

He quirks a brow. "Do you not want me to be here?"

I blink a few times, mouth agape. "I-uh . . . I just wasn't expecting it."

But yes, I want you here. I missed not seeing you.

Not that I'd ever admit that out loud. Holy hell, I sound so stupid and desperate.

He sits on the edge of my bed, looking far too comfortable. "I need the notes from class, and I wanted to see you."

"Oh." The words come out barely a whisper as my cheeks flush, my gaze dropping to his lap where . . . I bite my lip, trying to suppress a moan. Unsuccessfully.

He chuckles, palming himself. "Hungry, Solnyshko? Want me to choke you with this cock and paint your pretty mouth with my cum?

I nod and drop to my knees, fumbling with his zipper. Apparently, fine motor skills go out the window when faced with Alexei's . . . everything. When I finally free him, I can't help but stare. He's hard, proud, already leaking, and my mouth waters at the sight. I waste no time swallowing him down, savoring the salty and musky taste that makes my dick throb.

Alexei fists my hair and sets a brutal pace as he starts to fuck my throat. "That's it. Take it all like a good little slut."

His words send shivers down my spine. I moan around him, my own neglected cock straining painfully against my jeans. I rut against nothing, desperate for friction.

"Fuck," Alexei hisses. "You gonna come just from sucking me off?"

I whimper in response, tears streaming down my face as I gag around his length. But I don't stop. I want to please him, want to make him feel good. Want to be good for him.

Alexei groans, his hips snapping forward as he holds my head in place. His cock hits the back of my throat, and I swallow around him. "Fuck, Eli." He growls, his fingers tightening in my hair. "You look so fucking perfect like this."

I hollow out my cheeks, sucking him hard as he chases his release. With a final thrust, he spills down my throat with a guttural groan. I swallow every drop, licking him clean as he pulls out of my mouth.

But I don't stop there. I trail my tongue down his length, licking and sucking at his balls. Alexei shivers, his breath hitching, and I can't help but feel a little smug.

That is, until I venture lower, and my tongue flicks out to taste the sensitive skin of his taint.

He goes rigid, then backs away from me with wide eyes, his chest heaving as he tries to catch his breath.

"Alexei?"

He runs a hand through his dark hair. "I-I'm not into that," he mutters, his voice gruff and uneven.

I sit back on my heels, wiping my mouth with the back of my hand. "I'm sorry. I didn't mean to make you uncomfortable."

He stands, then pulls up his pants. He steps around me and starts pacing, rubbing his hands over his face, mumbling to himself in Russian. He shakes his head then looks at me. "I like what we do, but I . . . don't think I'm gay. I can't be."

His words hit me like a punch to the gut. Not again. This might be worse than the Great Tinder Catastrophe because I actually like Alexei. But it looks like I'm just another experiment.

Again.

Except he's growing more frustrated, yanking at the roots of his hair, growling. I step toward him, placing a hand on his arm. "Alexei?"

He stops pacing, eyes narrowing, a muscle near his jaw twitching. "How can I be gay if I don't like being touched there? If I don't want to be touched there?"

Oh.

Ohhh.

I bite my bottom lip and take his hand into mine, hoping it offers him some comfort, then take a deep breath, choosing my words carefully. "Being attracted to men doesn't mean you have to engage in anything that makes you uncomfortable. It's about who you're attracted to, not what you're comfortable doing in bed. There are plenty of men in relationships who don't engage in penetration."

He's silent but some of the tension leaves his body, his shoulders relaxing. But he still looks confused, uneasy.

"Sexual orientation is more fluid than just gay or straight, and there's no rush to figure things out, okay?" I reassure him, my voice soft. "We can take things slow, at your pace. And if you want to leave, that's okay too. I won't be upset."

He looks at me, his dark eyes searching mine, then shakes his head. "No. And I do need to copy the notes from class."

I walk to my desk and grab my notebook. When I turn back around, Alexei has made himself comfortable on my bed and is flipping through my sketchbook, his brows furrowed in concentration.

I can't help but smile, shaking my head as I walk over to him. "Pretty sure that's not what you're here to study."

He just grunts, continuing to thumb through the pages. I flop down on the other end of the bed to give him space, but he looks up, glaring. Before I can react, he reaches around my waist and pulls me close so I'm sitting between his legs, my back to his chest.

"Thank you," he murmurs, the words muffled against my hair.

"For what?"

"Being patient." His voice is gruff, but there's a vulnerability there that makes my heart do a little flip. "I've never . . . been physical with a man before. It's all new."

I relax into him, warmth blooming in my chest. "We'll figure it out together."

As Alexei's arm tightens around me, I can't help but wonder where this is going. It's messy and complicated and probably a terrible idea. But right now, with his solid warmth at my back and his breath on my neck, I can't bring myself to care.

Alexei

CHAPTER TWELVE

My blades carve the ice as I weave through the pathetic defense, my pulse thrumming with the high of watching these losers scramble and fail to keep up. I catch the scoreboard from the corner of my eye. We're crushing Sacred Heart 3-2.

It's a vicious bloodbath tonight but I'm dialed in, allowed off my chain to fully unleash on these hapless bastards. I smash another gutless winger into the boards.

Fuck yes.

His agony is my symphony.

"Petrov's out for souls tonight." Walsh's voice carries over the carnage. "These bitches will be lucky to leave breathing."

I bare my teeth in a sinister grin as the ref's whistle blows. The fool on the ice gets helped to the bench while I glide over to my laughing teammates.

Jackson claps me on the back. "I think your wet dream is making snow angels in piles of entrails."

"Save some for the rest of us, yeah?" Knight pins me with a glare. "Hate getting stuck with your boring leftovers."

I crack my neck, hungry for the next wave. "If your limp-wrists can keep up, I'll gladly leave scraps to gnaw on."

Jackson smirks. "Any of this have something to do with whatever new toy you're playing with? You know, since you're coming in at ass o'clock every morning."

"When do you ever notice what time I get in?"

"Fuckhead, you've stopped roaring at me for waking your cranky ass up. So, who's the tragedy letting you wet that sad dick on the regular?"

"None of your business."

"Getting your knob polished has you downright pleasant. She got a sister?" His eyes glint eagerly, ever the prowling tomcat. "I'll play nice if there's a chance for twins."

"Find your own holes to crawl inside." My smile holds no mirth, only teeth. "This one's not to be touched."

Though I turn my focus back to the game as we retake the ice, my thoughts drift unexpectedly to flushed alabaster skin marked by my mouth, to the symphony of desperate cries as I jerked our cocks off last night, and to how he screamed my name as I fingered his—

"Petrov! Too many men!"

Fuck.

I shake off the distracting memories and hurry to the bench before we catch a penalty. Don't know what my cousin's experience was like the first time he realized he was into men, but Eli's been patient over the two weeks, explaining things, and letting me figure shit out. Grateful for that in more ways I can ever explain.

Back on the bench, I down half my water bottle and force myself to focus. I can indulge in memories of my solnyshko later. Right now, I need to concentrate on the game.

Prove to the scouts I'm worth taking a chance on.

Two minutes later, I'm back out as we kill a penalty, paired with Walsh and Knight. We fall seamlessly into familiar roles—Knight harrying the puck handler, Walsh blocking shooting lanes while I wait to exploit any opening.

Viktor bats away a blistering slapshot and mock yawns. "My dead grandmother's got harder shots!"

Walsh gets away with hacking one of their forward's ankles. Love when the refs turn a blind eye. Though, it's more likely they're just too slow to notice.

Knight swoops in, poke checking the puck away. He zips a crisp pass my way and I'm off, blowing past flat-footed defenders. Their goalie scrambles as I close in, winding up for the kill.

A perfect snapshot sails just out of his despairing glove, bulging the twine behind him, and the stadium erupts in thunderous cheers.

This game is over before it even started.

By the final horn, I've scored once more and assisted on two others. We steamroll Sacred Heart: 7-3.

For the first time since finding out I didn't make the draft, I feel like making it to the NHL is truly possible.

Eli

CHAPTER THIRTEEN

The roar of the crowd still hums in my ears as I push through the heavy doors of Crestwood University's hockey rink. A gust of cool air hits my face like a slap, and I pull the collar of my jacket up to protect my ears as I get jostled by students pouring out of the arena.

I can't believe I just watched my first hockey game. And not just any game—Alexei's game. It was exhilarating. The raw energy, brutal hits, and speed on the ice—nothing like anything I'd ever experienced before. The crowd, decked out in maroon and gold, felt like one giant, roaring beast feeding off the violence of the game.

I sat way up in the stands, trying to stay hidden, unsure how Alexei would react to me being there. Sure, we've been spending more time together, even exchanged phone numbers—well, he demanded mine—but things between us are still frustratingly unclear. It's like a Jackson Pollock painting—colorful, chaotic, and open to interpretation.

But none of that mattered as I watched him play. Alexei was a force out there, a predator on the ice. Every move he made was precise, powerful, like he was born for this. The way he controlled the puck, the way he anticipated his opponents' moves, the sheer aggression in his every stride—it was mesmerizing.

And terrifying.

And hot as hell.

I shake my head, trying to dislodge the image of him slamming some poor guy into the boards. It should repulse me but, instead, it sends a strange thrill through me. I'm so screwed.

As I cut across the lawn, heading back to my dorm, I spot Sasha and Winston by a lamppost. Sasha's arms are crossed, her dark curls bouncing slightly in the breeze, while Winston stands with his hands stuffed into his pockets, his glasses catching the streetlight.

My face heats up as I approach, already knowing what's coming. I bite my lip and keep my head down. "Hey, guys."

"Uh, huh." Sasha raises a perfectly sculpted eyebrow, her eyes boring into mine. "Since when do you care about sports, let alone hockey? You nearly had a stroke when I suggested watching the Super Bowl last year."

I shrug, shoving my hands into my pockets. "I, uh . . . just thought I'd try something different."

Winston pushes his glasses up his nose and frowns. "Eli Holmes, lover of all things art and hater of all things sports, voluntarily attends a hockey game? Something's fishy."

I roll my eyes and huff. "It was just one game, guys. No big deal."

Sasha opens her mouth, but Winston jumps in first, bouncing on his toes and pulling his shoulders in. "Can we do this somewhere warmer? I'm losing feeling in my toes, and I'd rather not freeze just to interrogate Eli."

I let out a quick breath, nodding fast, glad for the momentary reprieve. "The Grind?"

Sasha perks up, and I know I've got her. Her barista crush will keep her occupied long enough for me to avoid the interrogation.

We speedwalk to the west end of campus, then cross the street to the cozy café that's our go-to hangout spot. The warm, coffee-scented air envelops us as we enter, and some of the tension leaves my shoulders. It's like being hugged by a giant, caffeinated teddy bear, made even cozier by the soft glow of string lights intertwined with fake cobwebs draping from the ceiling.

The place is packed with students fresh from the game, those who aren't heading straight to a bar or a keg party. We weave through the crowd to the counter that's lined with jars of candy corn, and Sasha leans in, her smile wide. "Hi! I'll have a grande caramel macchiato, extra hot."

The barista grins, dimples appearing in his cheeks. "Coming right up. Anything else?"

I order a chai latte and a cranberry scone, while Winston opts for hot chocolate. Sasha sends us to find a table while she waits for our order, clearly planning to flirt with the barista.

Winston and I grab a table near the back, settling into the worn velvet armchairs. He stares at me, his knee bouncing under the table, but stays silent as I pull off my jacket.

A few minutes later, Sasha shows up with our order, placing the tray down on the table. She slides into the chair, eyes locked on me. "Alright, Eli. Spill. And don't give me any 'I just wanted to check it out' crap. You've been MIA lately, and now you're at a hockey game? What's going on?"

Winston grabs his mug of hot chocolate, then leans back into the chair. "Yeah, man. We've barely seen you."

I take a bite of my scone, avoiding eye-contact. "I've just been busy with my sculpture project."

Sasha leans forward, her eyes narrowing. "Uh-huh. And does this 'sculpture project' have anything to do with why you're suddenly into hockey?"

Winston narrows his eyes behind his glasses and then reaches across the table, gently tugging at my shirt collar. "Is that a hickey?"

My hand shoots up to my neck, face burning. Damn it. Alexei's been getting a little . . . enthusiastic with marking lately. And as much as it's ridiculously possessive, it also turns me on in ways I can't even explain.

Sasha gasps, eyes wide. "Oh my god. You're seeing someone!"

I squirm in my seat, fidgeting with my mug. "It's . . . nothing."

"Nothing?" Sasha scoffs. "Eli, you've been practically celibate since The Great Tinder Catastrophe. And now you're walking around with a hickey? Who is he?"

I practically start gulping down the latte, even if it's too hot. I'd rather deal with a burnt tongue right now.

Winston's eyes widen, his mouth agape. "Oh, no. Don't tell me."

Sasha turns and looks at Winston. "Who?"

Winston shakes his head then locks eyes with me. "Is it Alexei?"

"What!" Sasha's voice booms and people at nearby tables turn to stare at us.

My cheeks and neck heat as I place my mug on the table. Turns out my silence and blushing are answer enough.

Sasha throws her hands up into the air, mumbling a string of curses. "Eli, are you insane? Have you forgotten how he treated you? How he beat up my ex-boyfriend last year?"

I pick at my scone, my jaw clenching. "You mean the ex who was stealing money from you and cheating with half the campus?"

She jerks back and blinks a few times. Dammit. I hadn't meant to hurt her feelings.

"Sorry." My voice comes out as a whisper.

Winston clears his throat and I turn my attention to him. "Eli, he's dangerous."

I bristle a little at their protectiveness, even though I know it comes from a place of love. "He's not as bad as you think. He's actually . . . kind of sweet sometimes."

The words feel strange as they come out, but they're true. Beneath all the aggression and intensity, there's a vulnerability to Alexei that no one else sees. I take a deep breath, the truth spilling out before I can stop it. "I think . . . I think I'm falling for him."

The café suddenly feels quieter, like the clatter of mugs and conversations has faded into the background. Sasha reaches across the table, squeezing my hand. "We're here for you, no matter what. Just promise us you'll talk if anything happens. Anything at all."

"I promise."

"And if he hurts you, Sasha will kick his ass," Winston adds with a smirk.

I laugh, shaking my head. "I'll keep that in mind."

Sasha rolls her eyes, sipping her caramel macchiato. "Alright, now that we're caught up on your love life, what about your art project? You've been tight-lipped about that too."

I pull out my phone, showing them a picture of the small-scale model I've been working on. "It's getting there. Still need to finalize some details, but I'm pretty happy with it so far."

"Wow." Winston leans in for a closer look. "That's incredible, Eli."

"Thanks," I say, a flush of pride creeping in. "It's still just the prototype, but I'm happy with how it's turning out."

As Winston and Sasha lean in to get a better look, my thoughts drift back to Alexei. I wish I could explain to them how he makes me feel—the spark when we touch, the way my heart races when he looks at me.

But underneath it all, there's still that nagging worry. What if this is just temporary? What if, once Alexei figures himself out, he realizes I'm not what he wants?

I focus back on my friend and on the way they look out for me, always checking in. Sasha and Winston keep me anchored when everything else feels like it's spinning. So, no matter what happens with Alexei, I know they'll be there for me, every step of the way.

Alexei

The glow from Eli's TV flickers across his face as we lie on his bed, some cartoon spy show playing in the background—*Archer*, he said. It's his favorite, apparently. I don't get it, but the way he laughs, eyes lighting up at every dumb joke, keeps me watching.

He's curled up against me, head resting on my chest, his breath hitching with every laugh. It's strange—this feeling, this . . . contentment. Never had it with anyone before, but it feels right.

Comfortable.

I glance down at him, taking in the way his dimples deepen when he grins, the flush on his cheeks when he's really amused. His hair's a mess—just how I like it—and his fingers absentmindedly toy with the hem of my shirt.

My fingers thread through his hair, and it's soft. He leans into my touch, just like a cat. Always craving more.

The episode ends, and Eli turns to me, that soft smile of his making his blue eyes brighter. "What do you think? Still not your cup of tea?"

I smirk, looking down at him. "It's growing on me, but I'd rather be doing something else right now."

His eyes widen a little, that blush creeping back onto his face. "Oh? Like what?"

I don't bother answering, just lean down and capture his mouth with mine. He tastes sweet, like the soda he's been sipping. I take my time, deepening the kiss, gripping the back of his neck, keeping him close—exactly where I want him.

He whimpers against me, hands fisting my shirt as he tries to pull me even closer. It's easy to flip him onto his back, pinning his wrists above his head. His breath hitches, arching his back as he gazes up at me, his cornflower blue eyes dark with desire. He's so fucking beautiful, and the way he's looking at me right now—like I'm the only thing he wants in the world—makes my chest tighten.

"Alexei . . ." His voice comes out in a whine, and I love it.

I chuckle, nipping at his ear. "So fucking desperate already?"

"Always for you . . ."

SAVAGE TITAN

When he tilts his head back, I take full advantage, sucking and biting at the sensitive skin. He squirms beneath me, his erection pressing against my thigh as he dry humps my leg like he can't help himself.

I let go of his wrists only to yank his shirt over his head. His chest is heaving, his breath coming in quick, shallow gasps. I dip my head, running my tongue over one of his nipples. He arches into me, a moan slipping past his lips when I bite down. Hard.

His hands grip my shoulders, nails digging in, but I grab his wrists and slam them back down above his head. "Told you to keep them there."

He whimpers but obeys, clasping his hands together above his head. The outline of his cock strains against his jeans, and I can't help but smirk as I unbutton them. "You're so hard for me, aren't you, Solnyshko?"

"Can't help it," he whispers, eyes hooded.

Slowly, I unbutton his jeans, sliding them down his hips along with his boxers. His cock springs free, already hard and leaking. I wrap my hand around him, stroking slowly, the heat from his skin burning into mine.

His hips buck into my touch, and his eyes flutter closed. "You like that?"

He nods frantically, moaning, body trembling with every stroke.

"Good. Because I'm just getting started."

115

I bite the inside of his thigh, hard enough to leave a bruise, and he yelps. I smirk, licking the spot before doing the same to his other thigh. His cock leaks even more, my own now straining against my jeans, but this—this is all about him.

About showing him how much he means to me, even if I can't find the words to tell him.

I drag my tongue up the length of his shaft, and Eli's whole body jerks. "Alexei, you don't have to . . . I mean, if you're not ready . . ."

I growl low in my throat, gripping his neck with one hand. "I want to. I want to taste you, to make you scream."

Eli's eyes flutter shut and he nods, falling back onto the bed after I release his throat. It's my first time doing this, but I'm determined to make it good for him.

I grip Eli's cock, clear liquid already dripping down his shaft, glistening in the dim light. My tongue darts out to lick it up, savoring the salty, musky flavor.

"Ohhh, God."

I chuckle, low and deep. "That's right. Keep calling me that."

Wrapping my lips around the swollen head of his cock, I swirl my tongue, teasing him mercilessly. He bucks, but I slam his hips down, pinning him in place. "Stay still."

I take him deeper, gag reflex be damned. Saliva spills from my mouth, coating his cock as I work him harder.

"Alexei, fuck, fuck." His tangles his fingers in my hair.

I pull off with a pop and slap the inside of his thigh. "What did I say about your hands?"

He whines, putting them back above his head, but the desperation in his eyes makes me grin.

"You like being sloppy for me, Solnyshko?"

"Yes . . . Please. Please, Alexei, more . . ."

I keep sucking him, and he gets louder, more desperate. Good. I want everyone to hear him. Let them know exactly who's making him fall apart.

His moans fill the room, and his cock swells in my mouth, his balls tightening. He's close, but I'm nowhere near done.

When I pull off, he whines, body trembling. "Alexei, please . . . I'm so close."

"Not done yet." I suck his balls into my mouth, rolling them gently with my tongue, and he lets out a strangled moan.

I grin, moving lower, licking a path from his balls to his hole. His legs tremble, spreading wider to give me better access. I don't hesitate, diving in with my tongue, tasting him, fucking him with it because I can't get enough of the way he tastes.

"Oh, fuck. Oh, fuck. Oh, fuck." Eli's cries echo around us as he grinds against my face. "Please. Please. Please."

I move back to his cock, taking him deep again. I suck him harder, my cheeks hollowing, my mouth working him as I grip the base of his cock and pump him.

He's thrashing, moaning, on the edge. "Alexei, I'm gonna—"

I lock my lips around him, greedy for everything he's about to give. He comes with a scream, spilling into my mouth, and I swallow every last drop, savoring the taste of him.

When he's done, when his body relaxes, I sit back, wiping my mouth with the back of my hand. He's sprawled out, flushed and wrecked, eyes glazed.

He's so fucking beautiful, and he's mine.

All mine.

I roll onto my back, wrapping my arms around him, and he snuggles against my chest, his body fitting perfectly with mine. I press a kiss to his head, breathing in his scent. This is where I belong. With him.

And I'm never letting him go.

Eli

CHAPTER FIFTEEN

I sit cross-legged on my bed, sketching aimlessly in my notebook.

For hours.

I don't even know how many I've completed, just that this rush of creativity has stemmed from the Russian asshat I'm falling for. The same one who flips through this darn book whenever he gets a chance.

Like it's his favorite thing to do outside of hockey.

I pull back for a second, glaring at the sketch, a tinge of jealousy inking its way into my blood.

Oh, hell. Am I really jealous of an inanimate object because I want to be Alexei's favorite thing to do outside of hockey?

Doesn't help that all my sketches seem to revolve around him in some way. As if he's my muse.

Ugh.

Muse. I sound like some old person from one of those ancient books they make us read in literature class.

One thing I am learning about myself is that my best work seems to come out when I'm emotionally invested in some way. And as of lately I've been emotionally invested in Alexei Petrov.

Speaking of . . . I want to get to know him more, outside of sex.

And there just so happens to be an art exhibit on campus tonight, showcasing students' work, including mine.

Maybe I should invite him.

Before I can overthink it, I grab my phone and shoot him a text.

> Hey, there's an art exhibit on campus tonight. Want to check it out with me?

My knee bounces as the minutes tick by with no response. Finally, three dots pop up.

> Why the fuck would I want to do that?

I roll my eyes.

Come on, big guy. Live a little.

Another agonizing few minutes.

Fine. I'll go to your stupid art thing.

I grin.

It's a date!

Immediately, I want to smack myself. Why did I use the word date? That implies a relationship . . . and I still have no idea what our situationship is. Only that 'I belong to him' as he likes to keep reminding.

Too late now, especially when 'read' appears below the text.

When he doesn't respond, I'm relieved and hurt. Didn't know both feelings could happen at the same time.

A few hours later, I'm fidgeting with my shirt collar, tugging it straight for the tenth time as I walk across campus to Crestwood University's Visual Arts Center.

My heartbeat is out of control the closer I get to the exhibit, and I'm sweating like a bison in heat, sure I'll pass out any moment.

There goes not making this such a big deal.

I spot Alexei leaning against the wall outside the gallery. In a suit. His wavy dark brown hair is perfectly coiffed back from his face. He exudes sex and power and dominance.

And here I am in a pair of khakis and a cornflower blue polo. I groan and slow down.

Only Mr-Sex-on-Two-Legs spots me, and I wipe my sweaty palms on my pants as I walk over to him.

When I reach him, his woodsy body wash mixes with his natural musk, assailing my senses and a pleasant shiver works its way down my spine. I shake it off and force a smile to hide my nervousness. "You made it."

He pushes off the wall, shoving his hands in his pockets. "Don't look so shocked. I said I would come."

"Well, thank you."

I grab the door handle and we walk inside. Alexei trails behind me, scowling at the colorful abstract paintings and imaginative sculptures. I give him tidbits about each piece, but his eyes remain stormy.

Then we reach my sculpture, *Unheard Melodies*, and his steps slow as he cocks his head, studying the abstract human figures crafted from clay, metal, and glass.

"This is yours?"

I nod, wetting my dry lips with the tip of my tongue. "I made it for my sister. She's deaf. The one on the left represents her, hands raised in sign language. The one on the right is the rest of the world, unable to understand her."

I trace my fingers over the clay, remembering the hours I'd spent researching sign language manuals to perfectly depict the hand positions. "It's how she described her childhood to me once. Feeling isolated even when surrounded by family."

"It's really good. You have a lot of talent." Alexei sweeps his gaze over the piece once more before meeting my eyes. "She's lucky to have a brother who sees her . . . truly sees her."

Unexpected tears gather, and my cheeks grow warm at the unexpected praise and empathy. "Thanks."

The tiniest of smiles plays on his lips. "Don't act so surprised. I can appreciate talent." The smile falls away. "Even if it's not related to hockey."

"Sorry I said that to you." I step closer, lowering my voice. "It's just . . . you know it doesn't make you any less of an athlete to have other interests."

He tenses. "Try telling that to my father."

"Well, your father isn't here right now. It's just me, and I like hearing about all the parts of you. Not just the hockey star."

Alexei takes hold of my hand, running his thumb along my knuckles. The simple, unguarded touch sends butterflies swirling madly in my stomach. "Thank you for showing me this."

"You're welcome." I can't stop the wide smile breaking across my face even if I wanted to.

We continue through the exhibit hand in hand as he lets me guide him from piece to piece, listening intently while I describe the artistic elements.

By the end, the ever-present tension in his broad shoulders has noticeably lessened. I chalk it up as a success.

As we exit into the cool evening air, Alexei turns to me. "Let's get something to eat."

"Sure." We end up at a diner just off campus. Once we order, an awkward silence settles between us. I fiddle with my napkin, searching for a conversation starter.

"So . . . am I the first guy you've ever been interested in?" I blurt out, then wince when he pales, looking down at the table. "Sorry, that just kind of came out. We don't have to talk about it."

I rub my hands over my thighs, as if trying to soothe the nervousness bubbling in me. Not just nervousness but . .

. jealousy too. I know he's never been with another guy, but maybe he's had crushes.

What if he's secretly been pining over a teammate?

He scrubs a hand down his face. " I just . . . I'm still figuring things out." He won't meet my eyes. "I've never felt this way about a guy before. Never felt much of anything for girls either. Hockey has always been my only focus."

"You don't feel desire?"

He snorts. "I do. But I wasn't talking about sex."

His brows furrow, features hardening. "Training and hockey are what I breathe. Relationships are . . . were distractions. Never wanted one before. Was never allowed to have one either."

"Never allowed?"

"My father had rules."

When he doesn't elaborate, I reach across the table and take his hand again. "There's no rush to label yourself. Or us. We can take things slow like we have been, figure it out together."

Except I can't help but focus on how he just said he never wanted a relationship before. Does that mean . . . .

Alexei turns my hand over, brushing his fingers over my knuckles like before. His eyes bore intensely into mine. "Promise me if I let you in, you won't use it against me, won't try to take my dreams away."

"I would never." I lace our fingers together. "I care about you, Alexei."

The waitress arrives with our food, forcing us apart. We eat in silence, my mind spinning. I can't imagine dedicating my life to something while forsaking the rest. And why would he ask me not to take his dreams away?

My eyes drift over Alexei. I've never seen him hesitant. Even the other night when he gave his first blowjob ever, he was all in.

But the concept of a relationship worries him, makes him nervous. Then again, it sounds like he's never had one before. And not by choice.

What kind of man raised him?

After we finish eating, Alexei walks me back to my dorm. When we come to a stop in front of my building, he shoves his hands in his pockets. "I had a nice time."

"Me too."

We stand there smiling at each other like idiots until I can't take it anymore. I grab the front of his jacket, pulling him down into a kiss, which he returns eagerly.

Alexei breaks the kiss and rests his forehead against mine, his eyes fluttering closed. "What are you doing to me, Eli?" His voice is a ragged whisper.

"I could ask you the same thing." I smooth back a lock of his dark brown hair. "I've never felt so connected to someone either."

He nuzzles against my neck, placing a soft kiss below my ear, and I cling to him, wishing we could stay like this forever. No expectations, no pressure to be anything but ourselves.

Alexei pulls back, clearing his throat gruffly. "I should go. Early practice tomorrow."

"Okay."

Except I don't want him to go. I want to drag him inside, curl up into his stupidly muscular body, and fall asleep.

But that's selfish.

So, I shove my hands into my pockets, shoulders slumping, and swallow the tiny whine threatening to escape as he walks away, disappearing into the night.

Oh, holy hell.

I'm in love with Alexei Petrov. Truly, madly in love.

Alexei

CHAPTER SIXTEEN

Walking along the cobblestone path leading back to my dorm, I rake my hand through my hair, letting out a long sigh. Sure, I've got practice in the morning. Makes logical sense to get some rest.

But every bone in my body screams to return to Eli.

The kiss didn't help much, but it's more than that. Sharing how his sister inspired that sculpture touched something deep in me, as if he is capable of seeing all of me too. Like he'll accept me for who I actually am, not what he wants me to be.

I won't deny how fucking good it felt when he called our outing a date. And damn if I don't ache to see his face, hear his voice, feel him pressed against me, to bury myself inside him permanently.

Turning back in the direction I came from, my boots eat up the sidewalk as my strides lengthen, and the few students in my path scramble out of my way.

Good, because if they hadn't moved fast enough I'd run them the fuck over. No one better keep me a second longer from getting to my Solnyshko.

My brows lift and I shake my head. Never been one to use terms of endearment toward anyone.

I knock hard on the door, my knuckles colliding aggressively with the hard surface, and when Eli opens the door, I shove him back as I step in, glancing quickly around the room. "You're alone."

Not that it would've mattered.

He doesn't say a word, just crashes his mouth greedily against mine. I groan, palming his ass and hauling our bodies flush. He's already hard and grinding against my thigh.

I need this maddening man like I need air.

Everything about Eli ignites me—his taste, his sounds, those clever fucking hands slipping under my shirt and mapping every ridge and valley of my chest.

I hiss as his palms glide over my abs. Breaking the kiss, I strip my shirt off and reach for his, desperate to feel his skin on mine.

When our bare chests meet, it's like pure, sizzling, unadulterated lightning.

"Off, get these off now," he says, fumbling with my belt and suit pants.

I chuckle, taking over and stripping out of my clothes as he does the same, though he's much less elegant about it. After, I fist my erection, groaning as I swipe my thumb over the leaking slit.

"Fuck, Alexei." Eli's blown pupils fixate on where I lazily stroke myself.

With a low snarl, I shove him onto the bed, then climb on top, bracketing him in. I watch his face intently as I grind down, our hard lengths sliding together.

Eli arches, mouth falling open as his eyes flutter closed. "Oh, God. Yes . . . need more . . ."

I lean down, biting and sucking across his throat and chest, laving his tight nipples until he's a writhing mess beneath me. His fingers dig ruthlessly into my skin, marking me as I rut against him.

Skating my lips up the salty skin of his neck, I nip sharply at his jaw to get his attention. "Open your eyes. Look at me. I want to see you."

As soon as his lust-blown gaze meets mine, I know. I'm going to claim every fucking inch of him tonight. Wreck him so thoroughly, there's no coming back for either of us.

Eli's cheeks flush even darker as he rocks up, seeking more contact.

"Need to be in you," I grit out, the urge to solidify our connection until all the blurred lines cement into one pulses violently through me.

"Are . . . are you sure?"

"Yes."

Propping himself up on both elbows, Eli nods toward the bedside drawer. "Grab the lube and a condom. I'll stretch myself open for you."

"No. Tell me what to do," I counter as I open the drawer, then reach into it, snatching up the bottle and a condom. "I've fucked a girl's ass once. Told you that."

Eli snorts. "Yes, you did it once. Now let me show you how it's really done. What I need."

He takes the lube from me, then slides farther up the bed, hiking one knee up and giving me an exquisite view of his hole as he drizzles lube over his fingers before circling his rim. Once done, he sinks a single digit inside with a soft hiss that has my fists bunching the sheets as if the action will somehow keep me here on Earth.

It's the most erotic thing I've ever witnessed. One finger becomes two, then three as he loosens himself up. His free hand trails up his torso to tweak a nipple before wrapping around his swollen cock.

I can't tear my eyes away, my erection now an angry red as I stroke myself in time with his fingers plunging steadily in and out.

Our gazes lock and something dangerous yet vulnerable passes between us. Carefully, I extract his fingers despite his needy whine and smooth the latex over my aching length, then slick myself up.

I want to wreck this man in the most profound ways imaginable, but uncertainty flickers in my chest. This step . . . having sex with him . . . My heart beats wildly. It'll be more than just physical.

"We can stop. We don't have to—"

"I need this." The confession rips its way free because this man owns me as irrevocably as I own him. "I need to fuck you until it's branded on your soul that every part of you belongs to me. Not anyone else. Me. And only me."

"Then take me." The blunt edges of his nails bite into my biceps as he tugs me down closer to him.

Gripping myself steady, I slowly press inside, breaching that tight furl of muscle. I groan loud. Eli's so tight. So warm.

When he rolls his hips, mine snap forward until I'm fully seated inside. When the rigid set of his muscles softens, I withdraw halfway, then sink back in until the slick sounds of our bodies moving together fills the room.

Eli whines, body squirming as he urges me on. "Come on, give it to me harder. Wreck me, Alexei."

A snarl rips from my throat as I grab his hips, angling us just right to nail his prostate on every punishing thrust.

"Oh, God. Fucking perfect. Yes," he chokes out, spine bowing as I nail that electric spot.

"This is my ass, my property. Fucking mine and only mine." I grip Eli's thighs, folding him nearly in half as I fuck into him like an animal. His pretty cock leaks ribbons across his clenched abs, and I can't resist wrapping my fingers around it.

"Yes, yes. Please, there. Fuck . . ."

I stroke downward, twisting just so as I tighten my grip.

"Oh, fuck Alexei . . ." His ass clamps down like a vise around me. "Your perfect dick's going to make me come so hard."

I'm close, that familiar pressure building in my balls, so I jerk him fast and rough, grunting against his skin. "Come on my cock then. Show me how good I fill your greedy hole."

Eli spasms, his cock erupting, cum striping his chest and abs. I bite down where his neck meets shoulder, fucking him through his orgasm as my vision whites out, and I come harder than ever before, every cell exploding in pleasure, then fusing back together, making me feel nearly invincible.

Through the fuzzy post orgasm haze, I just make out the sound of the door opening and turn my head. Eli's roommate stands at the threshold, gaping before slapping a hand over his face. "Oh, Jesus fuck. I live here too!"

He stumbles back out, pulling the door forcefully closed behind him.

I growl at the intrusion but Eli just dissolves into giggles.

His sleepy unfocused gaze finds me again, brighter than sunlight through rain clouds. "Maybe we should stay in your room sometimes."

"Or I'll just buy a bolt lock so the fuck can't get in." I slip free of Eli's pliant body to deal with the condom. His thighs tremble in the aftermath and he hisses slightly as I ease off the bed.

"Alexei, not happening. And be nice."

I turn my head and stare at him, brow raised. Me? Nice? But he just narrows his eyes in challenge as he finishes wiping himself clean with tissues.

Returning to the bed, I get in and pull him against me under the sheets. He immediately slings an arm over my waist, face nuzzling into my chest as I stroke my fingers up and down his spine. "Fine. Jackson's hardly around anyway."

We lay there in silence and his breathing slows, body going slack. "Love you, Alexei."

My chest seizes and I swallow hard past the lump lodged in my throat. I look down and his eyes are closed. Most likely, he doesn't even know what he just said.

I only hope he knows the depth of what I cannot yet voice because I think I love him too.

Eli

CHAPTER SEVENTEEN

Alexei's G-Wagon purrs smoothly down the dark, winding road, the headlights cutting through the cool October night. I've never been in anything even remotely close to this level of luxury before. I can't help but run my fingers over the buttery soft, black leather, marveling at its smoothness. It's a far cry from the worn fabric seats of my beat-up Corolla.

"You can relax, you know," Alexei says, a hint of amusement in his voice. "The seat won't bite."

I realize I've been sitting ramrod straight, barely letting my back touch it. "Sorry, I just . . . I've never been in a car like this before. It's a bit intimidating."

His chuckle is low and warm, making my heart skip a beat. "It's just a car, Solnyshko."

I raise a brow, gesturing to the dashboard, the touch screen, the ambient lighting. "Just a car? This thing probably costs more than my entire college education."

His lips twitch into a half-smile. "Probably. But it's still just a means of getting from point A to point B."

I shake my head, smiling. "Says the guy driving it."

Looking back out the passenger window, I fidget with a loose thread on my jacket sleeve, twisting it between my fingers, as if by doing so I can somehow unravel the knot in my chest. I should be thrilled Alexei's taking me on a surprise date.

But all I can think about is what came out of my stupid mouth four days ago.

Did he even hear me mutter "Love you" or had he already fallen asleep? He hasn't mentioned it, and if anything, he's been acting more like a boyfriend than ever. That's something I should be happy about, right?

I mean, we had sex. And not only did he initiate, the things he said, the way he needed me . . . he has no idea how much I do belong to him. I don't want anyone else.

Alexei's phone pings, breaking the silence. He checks it, his face hardening instantly, the sharp line of his jaw tightening as his grip on the steering wheel tightens, his knuckles turning white.

"Everything okay?"

He grunts, eyes flicking back to the road. "It's nothing."

"Doesn't look like nothing."

He sighs, his shoulders rising and falling heavily. "My father. He watched one of my games this week. Decided to tear apart my performance. Again."

"He was here?"

"No. He wouldn't have wasted the effort. Watched online, then sent me a list of all the ways I could've played better."

My heart aches for him. I've seen how hard Alexei works, how much pressure he puts on himself. "But you've been playing amazingly. I mean, I don't know much about hockey, but I see how talented you are."

He snorts, but there's no humor in it. "Tell that to him. Nothing's ever good enough."

I slide my hand over to his thigh, feeling the hard muscle beneath the fabric of his jeans. "Hey, look at me."

He glances over, his dark eyes stormy.

"You're incredible, Alexei. On and off the ice. And if your father can't see that, it's his loss." I gently squeeze his leg. "I see you, okay? All of you. And you're more than enough."

He lets out an audible breath as one of his hands slides off the steering wheel to cover mine, intertwining our fingers. "Thank you, Solnyshko."

We drive in comfortable silence for a while, the lights of Long Island blurring past us. Finally, he turns onto a smaller road, and I spot a sign for Old Bethpage Restoration Village.

"Where are we going?"

Alexei's lips curve into a smile. "You'll see."

As we pull into the parking lot, my eyes widen. Thousands of Jack O' Lanterns flicker in the darkness, casting an ethereal glow over the historic buildings.

"Alexei . . ." I have no other words for a moment as I take in the sight. "This is . . . wow."

He parks the car and turns to me, the soft light from the lanterns dancing across his face. He looks proud, yes, but also . . . vulnerable, like he's waiting to see if I'll love this place.

I lean over, cupping his face in my hands, then kiss him softly. "Thank you."

He growls low in his throat, deepening the kiss for a moment before pulling back. "Come on. Let's go see some pumpkins."

Hand in hand, we wander through the village, each turn revealing something more magical—a sea serpent made entirely of pumpkins, a carousel glowing with flickering lights, a giant clock tower carved with intricate detail. I can't stop pointing things out, my excitement bubbling over.

"Look at the way they've layered the carvings to create depth." I gesture excitedly at a particularly intricate design. "And the use of different sized pumpkins to build these structures—it's genius!"

He chuckles, pulling me closer. "You're cute when you're excited about art."

I blush, leaning into him. "Sorry, I'm probably boring you with all this technical talk."

"Not at all. I like seeing your passion."

Before I can respond, a voice cuts through the night. "Well, well, well. What do we have here?"

Alexei tenses beside me, his grip on my hand tightening as a tall, lean guy with ice-blue eyes and a mischievous grin saunters toward us. "What are you doing here?"

The guy waves a haphazard hand in the air. "Can't a guy enjoy some festive fall fun?"

"Bullshit." Alexei's eyes narrow at him.

"Well, I had to see where my cousin kept disappearing to. I was worried." The guy turns and looks at me, his head slightly tilted. "Wait, is this the one that had you all twisted up at Walsh's party a month and a half ago?"

Alexei's jaw clenches, but he turns to me. "Eli, this is my cousin, Viktor."

My eyebrows shoot up. "The one you talk about?"

Alexei nods, his body still tense. I glance back at Viktor, who's smile has morphed into outright glee, like he just got to meet Santa Claus in real life. "You were talking about me?"

I chuckle, surprised at how happy the guy is. "Alexei didn't mention you went to school with us."

Viktor's eyes narrow on his cousin. "Guess he didn't tell you I'm the Titan's goalie either."

"Really? Are you the one who made that split save a few weeks ago?" I cringe the moment the words leave my mouth. Why can't my stupid mouth keep quiet?

Alexei stares at me, eyebrow quirked. "You've been to my games?"

I bite my bottom lip, my neck and cheeks heating as I nod.

His eyes narrow. "I haven't seen you."

My face is on fire now and I look down at the ground, digging the toe of my Vans into the dirt. "I sit up high in the bleachers. Wasn't sure if you wanted me there."

Viktor breaks out into a laugh so loud the people around us stare as his gaze flicks between us. "Holy shit. Are you two dating?"

I stiffen, clamping my mouth closed. While we act like we're dating, we haven't actually defined what we are.

I look up at Alexei, unsure how to respond. We haven't really defined what we are, and I don't want to assume anything.

Alexei grabs my chin, forcing me to look at him, his dark eyes boring into mine. "Why'd you react like that?"

I swallow hard, avoiding his gaze. "I . . . I'm not sure how to answer."

Alexei's expression darkens. "What do you mean, you're not sure how to answer?"

I avoid his gaze, my cheeks burning as hot as lava. "I just . . . I didn't know if we were . . . you know, official."

Alexei's grip on my chin tightens. "What did you think I meant when I said you were mine?"

My heart races at his words. It's what I've wanted to hear, but I've been too afraid to hope for. "I hoped it meant we were dating," I say, my voice soft.

A low growl rumbles in Alexei's chest. "You're mine, Eli. My boyfriend. Is that clear enough for you?"

I nod, unable to keep from smiling. "Crystal clear."

Alexei's lips crash into mine, hard and demanding. My brain short-circuits, and I melt into him, my hands fisting in his jacket as his tongue sweeps into my mouth.

Viktor clears his throat, interrupting the moment. "So . . . a boyfriend, huh?"

Alexei pulls back, his hand tightening around mine. "He's my boyfriend." He takes a deep breath, his voice barely above a whisper. "And . . . I'm bisexual."

I squeeze his hand, silently offering my support. It's a huge step for him, admitting it out loud, especially to his family. He's figuring himself out, coming to terms with who he is, and I'm honored to be a part of it.

Viktor claps Alexei on the shoulder. "Well, well. Who would've thought my grumpy bear of a cousin would end up with such a cutie?"

Alexei growls, shoving Viktor away. "Shut up."

I smile at their interaction, at seeing Alexei in a different light once again. His cousin is so different from him, but their bond is evident.

Viktor laughs, turning back to me. "To answer your earlier question, yes that was me making yet another ESPN highlight worthy save."

Alexei grumbles, but I ignore him. "Are you hoping to make it to the NHL too?"

Viktor's smile turns a bit smug. "Already been drafted by the Islanders, actually."

"Wow, that's incredible. But . . . why aren't you playing for them now?"

Alexei snorts, rolling his eyes. "Because he wants to get an education."

I ignore Alexei's tone, genuinely curious. "What are you studying?"

"Chemical and Molecular Engineering," Viktor replies, puffing up a bit.

Alexei scoffs. "Yeah, he's a real genius. One who apparently can't see his presence is obviously not wanted."

"Says the dumbass who didn't bother to let his boyfriend know they were official." Viktor turns back to me, grabbing my hand and pulling me down the trail. "Come on, let's go see some more pumpkins, new bestie."

I look over my shoulder and catch Alexei rolling his eyes, muttering something under his breath about his cousin hijacking the date. Viktor ignores him and peppers me with questions about my classes, how his cousin went from wanting to kick my ass to kissing me, and wanting to know exactly what Alexei says about him.

As we move on to the next display, Alexei pulls me close, pressing a kiss to my temple. "Sorry about him."

"I'm glad he showed up. It's fun seeing you two banter. And he's charming."

Alexei grunts. "Don't say that too loud. The fucker needs way too much attention."

I snuggle into the side of his large body. He twists and lifts my chin, his eyes locking with mine. "You okay, though?"

I smile up at him, my heart full. "Never better."

Alexei

I shoulder open the locker room door, muscles pleasantly sore and sated after a hard practice. The team is on fire and there's no way we aren't going to make it to the Frozen Four. We'll dominate like we're meant to.

And I've been playing my best ever. Making it to the NHL isn't just a pipedream I'm holding on to. I can feel it in my bones.

Eli should be in the lobby or close by. He sent a text that he was grabbing coffee and wanted to walk to class together.

Guess my teammates are about to find out where I've been spending my spare time. Unless my cousin already opened his big mouth.

I'm barely two steps into the lobby when I spot a familiar imposing figure and halt dead in my tracks.

No chance I'm imagining Vladimir Petrov standing here as if summoned straight from the depths of hell itself.

"Father. I wasn't expecting you."

His piercing gaze rakes over me, cold and assessing as always. "You should have. I told you I would come to review your progress in person."

I bristle at his tone but bite back a sharp retort. I know better than to poke the bear. Learned that lesson the hard way. My finger skates over the faint scar along my left cheek.

"I attended your game against Cornell last month. Sloppy handling, inaccurate passing, completely ineffective checking. Your leg may have healed, but the rest . . . I had to leave after the second period before people realized you're my son." His lip curls and his eyes blaze with disgust.

"Are you fucking kidding me?"

His mouth tightens, gaze glacial. "Mind your volume, boy. I'll not be shouted at by my own blood."

"I've been kicking ass all season since that one game. Top ranks in assists, goals scored, time on attack—or do you even follow my stats?"

He just pins me with a glare, not answering.

"You know what, I'm fucking done. You're the reason I broke my leg—or did you forget? You almost stole my dream from me. *My* dream."

Movement over my father's shoulder catches my eye. Eli stands frozen a few feet away, a cup of coffee clutched in each hand.

I hadn't shared with him how I broke my leg. How my father was too busy swinging at me while driving and we got into a car accident. All because I was playing a game on my phone instead of immediately analyzing all the wrong moves I made on the ice earlier. He blamed my mediocre performance on that rather than the fact I'd been sick with a fever.

My father turns and looks over his shoulder. His gaze rakes across Eli as he lets out a dismissive snort. "This is how you choose to spend your time, with this worthless distraction?"

"You might be my father but Eli is mine."

My father turns back to me, one eyebrow ticking up. "Yours?"

"Mine." I straighten to my full height. "I love him, and I won't let anyone hurt him, not even you."

His thin lips curl again as he turns back to me. "My son's a cocksucker now? Ugh, just like your cousin."

I step closer, the two of us nearly nose to nose as we stare each other down. "Say one more fucking word. I dare you."

He lets out a snarl, then swings, his fist connecting with my cheek. The blow knocks me back one step, fire blooming where his ring splits my skin.

For the second time in my life.

I swipe my fingers over the cut as I stand tall. If he wants me cowed, I'll gladly disappoint him yet again.

Only Eli drops the coffee and rushes over, shoving my father away. "Don't you fucking touch him."

I push Eli behind me, not wanting my father to lay a hand on my Solnyshko.

But my father simply pulls a monogrammed handkerchief from his suit pocket and dabs at flecks of blood marring his gold ring with exaggerated care.

When he finishes, he pins me under frigid scorn once more. "Consider your accounts cut off as well as your tuition. And feel free to go cry to your aunt. She's used to little cock sucking bitches."

With that, he pivots on one polished loafer and stalks toward the exit, not sparing me another glance. Dismissing my entire existence as casually as trading a faulty appliance.

Silence follows until Eli brushes a warm hand along my forearm. "You're bleeding."

"Don't look so tragic. I'll be fine." At his doubtful stare I squeeze the slender fingers curling around mine. "Truly. I get hurt worse in hockey."

He grimaces and I chuckle.

"You know my plan is to play in the NHL. Did you think I would never get hurt?"

His eyes are wet. "That's . . . different, and I don't want to think about that right now. Your father just hit you, made you bleed. The things he said."

Maybe his words should hurt, but they don't. Not when he targets my cousin, or Eli. Instead, I want to kill him. To end him the way my aunt should have.

I tug him closer, arms winding snug around his waist as I brush a soft kiss to his temple. "As long as he didn't hurt you, I'm okay."

"But he cut you off. Your tuition."

"Idle threats. My mother's the one with the power. That prick just married into the family."

Vladimir Petrov better enjoy the little time he has left. There's a reason my mother stopped her sister from pulling the trigger that day. A business reason, not love. But she warned him about laying a hand on me, and Yulia Petrov is not one for idle threats.

Eli pulls back a little and looks at me. "I'm glad you stood up for yourself." He nibbles his bottom lip. "Did you really mean what you said? About . . ."

"I meant every word. You're my whole heart, Solnyshko." I kiss him tenderly, hoping my soul-deep emotions somehow transmit through.

"What does Solnyshko mean? You've called me that a few times."

I huff out a small laugh. "Closest translation is sunshine."

His lips form my favorite awed little 'O' shape, and my damn chest expands with emotion until I think I'll burst. There's no denying I've fallen truly, madly in love with this man who unravels me effortlessly.

My perfect counterbalance.

"I love you, Eli Holmes. All that I am is yours. You are everything to me."

"I love you too," he whispers against my neck. "Exactly as you are."

Eli

CHAPTER NINETEEN

My teeth sink into the side of my cheek as I chew the skin, my pace increasing as I make my way to Alexei's dorm. He should be back from his away game. Sure, it's only been one day but I miss my Russian bear.

I also need him right now because I'm freaking the hell out. I've been working on a new piece for class. Inspiration finally hit me, even if it came from one of the worst experiences I've ever been through.

Watching the showdown between Alexei and that biggest piece-of-shit-excuse-of-a-father broke my heart. And infuriated me. I still can't believe Alexei just shrugged off the fact his father punched him.

As it turns out, it's not the first time.

I'm not a violent person, but for once I wish I was as much of a psychopath as his friends are. I want to kill the bastard, to gouge his darn eyeballs out with a teaspoon. I think that would hurt. I hope it would.

But seeing Alexei, really seeing him, inspired my newest creation—a half torso with a tough as steel face where half the face shatters, revealing a secondary face full of hurt and pain and scars underneath.

Only my miniature model went missing, hence why I'm freaking out. The piece is due in two days, part of a benchmark grade for the larger project. How am I going to explain this to my professor?

I knock rapidly on his door, running my fingers through my hair, trying to fix what I can to not look as frazzled as I feel.

The door swings open and he doesn't even say hi. Nope, he just slams his mouth down onto mine and drags me inside as his tongue invades me. And I melt the way chocolate does in a car during the heat of summer, whining like I always do for him.

"Missed you, Solnyshko."

"I missed you too."

He pulls back a little, hand running along the side of my face, brows pinched. "What's wrong?"

I huff, about to ramble on about my missing miniature when I spot the damn thing on *his* desk.

My eyes narrow mere slits. I want to pummel the jerk. "Are you serious right now?"

"What?"

I point at the miniature sculpture. "That! I've been looking everywhere for it! Freaking the hell out and *you* have it!"

He shrugs, like it's no big deal. "Came by to surprise you this morning because we got home early but you weren't there. I saw it and thought it was beautiful and wanted it."

I step back and throw my hands up. "You unbelievable asshole. That's part of my grade, not for you to steal."

Some of my anger deflates when the fact he called the piece beautiful finally registers.

"First, I didn't steal it." He stands to his full height, crossing his arms. "And second, what did you just call me with that smart mouth?"

"If the shoe fits." My boyfriend has another thing coming if he believes I'm not going to call him out just because I love him. "Ask next time if you want something."

"Where's the fun in that?" His eyes darken and the corner of his mouth rises a little. "Maybe I should take my gift back and not give it to you."

My jaw drops, all previous frustration evaporating, as I involuntarily let out a rushed breath, like I've been punched in my chest - but in a good way. "You got me a gift?"

He juts his chin at the box sitting on his bed. I walk over, lift the lid, and gasp as I take out a sweatshirt. It's custom made in my favorite shades of blue and purple. Alexei's number, 44, is on the back and sleeves while the Titans logo is on the front.

"Why can't you just let me be mad at you for five minutes?" Tears prick the corners of my eyes as I hug the sweatshirt to my chest and smile wide. "Thank you. I love it."

"Sasha helped me get it made for you. My boyfriend should wear something special, something only he has instead of a jersey like everyone else."

I'm not sure what I'm more amazed by right now—the custom clothing he made for me in my favorite colors or the fact he planned this with one of *my* friends, who by the way did not let on that she was secretly working on this with him.

Alexei threads his fingers into my hair from behind, then yanks at the roots, my head jerking back as I gasp, dropping the sweatshirt.

He starts to remove my belt. "Don't think I forgot about you calling me an asshole."

"I'm so—"

"Shut up." He yanks the leather through my belt loops, then shoves the strap into my mouth, buckling it tight behind my head. "All I want to hear from you are those filthy sounds as you come on my cock."

My eyelids flutter as I moan loud. When did I turn into such a masochist?

"Arms up."

I lift them and he removes my shirt, then thrusts me down onto the bed, yanking the rest of my clothes off. When I'm fully naked, he flips me onto my stomach, tightly binding my hands behind my back with his belt.

The sound of his zipper catches my attention and I twist to look back. Alexei sheds his clothes and I pull my knees under me, arching my ass in the air and spreading my legs.

He chuckles, then slaps my ass hard, the sting radiating like some heavenly yet hellish fire. "I forget how needy you get for me."

His palm cracks down on my ass again. And again. And again. Stronger and more brutal each time.

My dick is hard and aching, twitching with each slap as I whimper into the leather. When I arch higher, pushing back, he tugs my balls and twists, and my dick drools precum.

Alexei spreads my ass cheeks wide, then runs his tongue up my entire crease. "Look at your greedy hole winking at me. So desperate for my cock."

I'm a mess of tears, letting out the filthiest, most desperate moans. Every inch of my skin is a center for arousal at this point.

"Need to fuck you, Eli. Need to come deep inside you."

I turn my head and look back at him. His expression is questioning. Every time we've had sex it's always been with a condom. We haven't talked about not using one.

But I need him to fill me, even if it might be the stupidest thing to do.

I nod and push back.

He groans, then gets off the bed to grab the lube, coming back and slicking himself and me up.

"Fuck, I love this ass." He slaps it again. "So beautiful all nice and red."

I'm a raw nerve of pleasure and pain as Alexei pushes into me, stretching me to capacity, filling me. Then he bends, his entire body covering mine, and fucks hard and fast.

It doesn't take long until I'm whimpering and writhing, needing him to touch my dick, to ease the ache. But he just pushes my head down into the mattress and fucks me harder, grunting like a wild beast in heat.

My breaths grow ragged, tears flowing freely down my face, every filthy sound coming out of me unrecognizable. And I love every minute of it.

Alexei's thrusts get more erratic, my own body is pushing back to meet his. "My desperate slut can't get enough of me. Fuck . . . Eli, I'm going to . . . Take my cum, baby."

The strangled sound he makes launches me into oblivion, and I start spurting without him touching my dick.

Then a wave of the most intense pleasure emanates from my asshole, contracting every part of me. I try to take a breath but can't, the sensation turning a little violent as it cascades throughout my body. And when Alexei moves, he only reignites the orgasm.

"Milk me, baby. Keep milking my cock."

After what feels like forever, my orgasm finally subsides and Alexei undoes both belts, then collapses onto the bed, pulling me tight against his chest. "Here I thought I was claiming you and your damn ass laid claim to me."

I nuzzle into him, too blissed out to think straight, and start to doze off when the door crashes open.

Alexei snarls as he grabs the blanket to cover us. "Jackson, get out."

Jackson's bored gaze slides over to me. "Figured you were his little toy."

"Watch how to talk to my boyfriend."

The sex bliss is gone, mushy love bliss taking its place. My heart flutters every time he calls me that, as if I'm hearing it for the first time.

I pick my head up. "Um, hi. I'm Eli."

Jackson just shrugs and flops onto his bed, unfazed. "The boy from Connor's party."

My brows furrow. "You knew it was me because I was at that party?"

Jackson rolls his eyes. "More like because *he* ran out of the party like his ass caught fire. Didn't look like he wanted to murder someone, more like he was running from something. Then you come from the same direction, looking all flushed, eyes glazed over. Seriously, it's simple math."

Alexei tenses beside me, and when I look up at him, he's death glaring his teammate.

"The showdown in the arena lobby spelled it out for any clueless idiot. Gotta say, Boy Toy, took guts standing up to Alexei's dad. Think I sorta might like you. Enough to not want to kill you at least."

"Be still my heart. Wouldn't want to ruin any of your homicidal tendencies." I snuggle closer into Alexei. "Are all your teammates like him?"

Alexei snorts. "Only the ones I can actually tolerate."

"Wonderful. So should I prepare to be arrested as an accomplice at some point?"

Alexei wraps his arm around me and kisses the top of my head. " Don't worry, I'll keep you away from trouble. Mostly."

I snort, quirking a brow. "Yet you let me hang around your cousin. And I can already tell he might be more trouble than you."

Jackson springs up, glaring at both of us. "What the actual fuck! Viktor knew! For how long? And hung out with him! Seriously, does our friendship mean nothing?"

Alexei takes his pillow and launches it at his roommate. "You and my cousin are so fucking whiny sometimes. But I'm surprised he kept his mouth shut."

Jackson tosses the pillow back then grumbles as he thumbs through his phone. After Alexei settles back in I let my eyes fall shut, perfectly content.

Who would've thought the love of my life would be the asshole who ran me down in the hallway two months ago.

Alexei

The crowd's deafening roar fuels my adrenaline as our skates carve across the ice. Games against the South Shore Serpents are the highlight of the season, for both the players and our fans. The rivalry between the two schools has gone on for generations.

Supposedly, that's common. When I came to Crestwood from Russia, Jackson and Walsh told me the North Shore and South Shore of Long Island are always at odds in every facet of life.

Walsh nods toward the stands. "Can't believe their fans are stupid enough to fill our stands."

I smirk. "Our fans are just as bloodthirsty for these fools as we are."

Jackson jerks his head toward where Eli sits. "You tell your boyfriend to be careful. You know whenever we play these dickwads, the fans fight too."

I look over to Eli, who's talking and laughing with his friends, wearing the sweatshirt I gave him. He looks good in that light blue he loves so much, and seeing my number on him settles something primal inside.

"If one strand of hair on his pretty little head breaks, I'll rip someone's throat out with my teeth."

No one better touch my sunshine if they know what's good for them, and they must because the only people sitting next to him are Sasha and Winston. Everyone's left a good three seat buffer around and behind them.

Smart.

I turn my attention back to the ice, my blood singing for destruction and violence. And no one brings that out of me more than Killian Blackwell.

Just thinking his name has my jaw ticking. That smug bastard and I have unfinished business, and I plan to leave him a bloody pile of broken bones by the time the final horn sounds.

The one person who wants to crush his soul more than me is Jackson. Their hatred is explosive. Turns Jackson dark. Darker than he already is.

Walsh wants to break him too, especially after Blackwell sent him headfirst into the boards last year.

We might love to coat the ice with blood, break a few bones, but we draw the line at brain injury type shit.

The first faceoff is brutal, players crashing and bashing like wrecking balls. No one holds back, blood spilling barely five seconds in.

Just how I like it.

I steal the puck, passing to Knight as I barrel down the boards. Blackwell moves to intercept, malice carved into his face.

Jackson slams into him. Before any of the Serpents can retaliate, I saucer the puck straight to Walsh's tape.

He dekes, buying time for me to cherry pick by the net. Walsh fakes the shot, then sends a blistering pass right on my tape where I let it rip.

Top fucking shelf where mama hides the cookies.

We're up 1-0 four minutes in. I make sure to flash Serpent's bench a grin and wink as I skate by.

During the second period, I assist on another goal while Knight turns one of the South Shore's wingers into his personal punching bag. Zach's last name might be Knight, yet my fucking friend is anything but.

Not sure what name would fit a sadistic psychopath.

In between shifts, I glance over at Eli, who gives me a subtle thumbs up that warms me straight down to my fucking soul.

During the third period, I finally draw Blackwell one-on-one. We battle, vicious and nasty, along the boards, trading hits.

My elbow comes up, crashing into his jaw. "Oops."

He spits blood and swings wild. The refs peel us apart and we both get matching penalties.

I blow Eli a dramatic kiss on my way to the box, and my boyfriend rolls his eyes. But I catch his little smirk. Yeah, he can pretend to be annoyed all he wants. I know better.

We pot two more goals before the final horn.

Titans triumph, 4-2.

I'm barely out of the locker room when familiar arms wrap around my waist. I sweep Eli into a blistering kiss, claiming him in front of everyone.

"So proud of you," he gasps when we separate.

"Love you, Solnyshko."

Eli smiles, soft and sweet. "Love you too."

A sudden commotion erupts nearby. Jackson and Killian are fighting like rabid animals, crashing into the walls while swinging at each other. They both end up on the ground, Jackson with the advantage as he pounds away at Killian's face.

The rest of the Serpents rush out of their locker room, heading straight for the rest of us.

Chaos explodes.

I pass Eli off to Viktor, knowing my cousin will keep him safe, then join the melee.

It's vicious, no refs holding us back now. Knight splits some idiot's forehead open before kicking his knees out. Walsh breaks another fool's wrist. Even one of our rookies body checks a Serpent into the vending machine, breaking the glass.

Beautiful destruction.

This is the Titan's kingdom, and we're going to remind these snakes why we rule this kingdom.

I find the nearest Serpent and smash his face into the wall. My cousin would be proud. It's his go-to move.

A hand clasps my shoulder—campus security. I surrender easily. They'll only hold us overnight to save face anyway.

I find Eli's worried face among the crowd. "Sorry, Solnyshko. Might be a late night. Have some vermin to take care of. Don't wait up, okay?"

He searches my face. I let him see the truth, all my jagged edges and seething violence. He just sighs. "Don't get into too much trouble."

I grin, wild and ruthless. "I make no promises."

As campus security drags me toward the exit, I spot Viktor slinging an easy arm around Eli's shoulders. My cousin's going to throw a tantrum later for being put on babysitting.

Too bad.

Viktor's the only one I really trust, even if he's a giant fucking headache most of the time.

Jackson scowls as he's led past me, and with a busted face and split knuckles, he looks every inch the nightmare we are.

A brutal Titan sent straight from hell to rain bloody retribution down on any who cross us.

I look at my boyfriend one last time and wink. While the Titans may own this town, Eli owns my fucking heart.

He's stuck with me until the day I stop breathing.

About the Author
E.V. OLSEN

E. V. Olsen is a romance author who loves to write about Over The Top alpha males who are possessive and completely obsessed with their person or mate. Nothing will get in their way from claiming what's theirs. E.V. enjoys writing darker or angsty type romances whether in the contemporary world, PNR worlds, and even post-apocalyptic worlds.

Connect with E.V. Olsen online

Website: https://evolsenbooks.weebly.com/
Tiktok: https://www.tiktok.com/@evolsenbooks
Instagram: https://www.instagram.com/evolsenbooks
Facebook: http://www.facebook.com/evolsenbooks

Also By
E.V. OLSEN

Wasteland Temptations Series
Mine to Claim (Book 1)
Mine to Protect (Book 2)
His to Break (Book 3)
His to Lead (Book 4)

North Shore Titans Hockey Series
Savage Titan
Brutal Titan
Unhinged Titan
Forbidden Titan
Ruthless Titan

Made in United States
Troutdale, OR
01/12/2025

27875163R10106